I0687132

Thank you...to ALL the first responders, firemen, law enforcement, emergency helpers, medical technicians, triage personnel, nurses, doctors, and bystanders (the list is endless) who are *the difference between life and death* in catastrophic accidents.

Whether responding to a train crash, a shooting, a wildfire, a plane crash, a terrorist attack, first responders and bystanders are the first ones on the scene. They perform their duties without a second thought on their own personal regard; they react, serve, and protect others in their time of need.

*Ashton James, Madelyn Rose,
Michaela Paige.... Mima loves
you with every breath!*

When your life leads up to
an event that leaves a
single experience etched
into your memory forever,
I call it the...

MOMENT
MOMENT
OF
IMPACT

Lindsay McDonald, thank you for taking this journey with me once again. Your covers, editing, formatting, graphic design—make me who I am. I only write the story....

Cynthia Rose, you're always there keeping my commas to a minimal. You rock!

Sue Ward and Philomena Callan (my UK reviewers), a special thank you for keeping me moving forward. As my Beta Readers, you always get the first peek at my new stories and your honesty humbles me!

# CHAPTER 1

## Chase

"Are you fucking kidding me, Bridge? What do you mean you won't be home until after your meeting this evening?" Chase Walker yelled through the kitchen door to his wife upstairs. "I have plans! You told me you would be home early!" His face was turning red, anger consuming him.

Bridget came running down the stairs, her tall, thin body and long legs taking the steps two at a time. Her blue eyes were narrowed when she popped her head into the kitchen. "Do you have to use that language around the kids? The boys are getting older and I don't want that garbage around them!"

"Did you hear what I just said? I have plans," he repeated defiantly, intentionally ignoring the daggers she was glaring at him.

Her fingers gripped the doorjamb. "I told you last week I had a very important meeting with a client. You said you'd marked it in your calendar."

"Well, I didn't!"

"Then that is your fault...not mine. Change your plans. I need to keep this meeting if you want to keep your golf membership to the club!"

"Don't threaten me...." His anger was building. He wanted to slam his fist into the wall, but the last time he had done that, he wound up in the hospital with a broken wrist.

"Change your plans. You can go hang with the guys next week." She flashed a condescending smile at his flushed face. "Honestly. And go take your blood pressure medicine. You look like you're about to blow a fuse."

"That's not fucking fair. Why can't you change your meeting?"

She sighed in exasperation. "Because we need this account if you want to continue to enjoy the lifestyle you love so much." With that said, again, her fingers let go of the doorjamb and she stalked back in to the large foyer, muttering under her breath, and placed the jackets of each of her four sons next to their lunch bags that she had packed the night before. Impatiently, she walked into the laundry room and placed the clothes from the washer into the dryer and turned it on. She loaded the washer with a pile of laundry that was laying on the floor. She turned and started walking back toward the stairs. With a quick detour, she popped her head back into the kitchen. "Do you really think I like these long hours and the after-hour business meetings, Chase?" Her lips were pursed, her eyes narrowed, and her white knuckles were gripping the doorjamb.

Chase crossed his arms over his chest and huffed. "I don't care if you do or if you don't! Tell your fucking father to take a hike! These long hours are cutting into our family time." He took a step toward her in anger, his voice growing louder. "I'm getting tired of picking up the kids from school and taking care of them until you get home. Three times this week I had to make dinner and I'm getting pretty pissed. When do I get time for myself?"

Bridget's jaw dropped and her eyes opened wide. "Time for yourself...? Didn't you go to Las Vegas with the boys a few months ago?" Bridget pointed a finger at Chase, her voice raising a few octaves. "I hate these long hours. How tired do you think I feel, barely making it through the door after fifteen hours of work? If you made a decent income that we could live on, I would gladly be a stay-at-home mother. But...seeing as my salary is three times yours, I don't have that luxury. We would starve to death." She turned to leave, then she suddenly turned around to look at him again, and said, "Let me know when I can quit my job. I'd be more than happy to give my father notice."

Chase slammed his hand down on the expensive granite counter. He growled in pain and started rubbing his palm. "You fucking bitch!"

Bridget narrowed her eyes again and hissed quietly so the kids would not hear. "If I'm a 'fucking bitch,' then why are you still here?" She waited for an answer, but did not get one. "Don't want to give up the comforts?"

Chase stood there and stared. You could almost see the jet of steam coming out of his ears.

Bridget turned around and her face was filled with resentment. "Oh, and before you start whining and complaining even louder...don't forget that Josh has baseball practice and Bryan has a dentist appointment!" Bridget smirked. She walked into the foyer again and yelled upstairs. "Okay, guys, it's getting late. You need to brush your teeth and come down for breakfast. We have to be out of here in ten minutes."

Bryan, Jax, and Dylan ran down the stairs and headed into the kitchen. Bridget counted only three heads, and asked, "Where's Josh?"

Bryan started to laugh and rolled his eyes. "Upstairs playing *Candy Crush!*"

Bridget yelled back upstairs, "If you aren't down in one minute, I'm taking away your cellphone. Do you hear me, Josh?"

"Okay, Mom, I'm coming down," he hollered back.

The upheaval of four young boys in the morning was beyond comprehension. The house had actually been in a state of chaos since Josh was born twelve years earlier. Then Bryan came two years later, Jax a year after, and Dylan was the baby at six years old. Dylan wasn't planned, but he was the quieter and most behaved of all their sons. Whether it was his passive personality or he had given up on competing with the older ones, there was no chance for him to shine with all the hostility around him.

Thirteen years of precarious balancing just to maintain a small shred of stability in the household…and lately everything seemed to be falling apart. With the steady stream of innuendos and never-ending arguments that Bridget and Chase threw at each other, the children were beginning to pick up the same dysfunctional behavior. Bridget didn't know how much more she could do or how much longer she could last working these horrendous hours. She resented it and would have liked to stay home to raise her sons. But it was not financially feasible. And it was

4

beginning to seem unfair that Chase was not pulling his share of the financial load.

Chase worked for a large construction company. He was their go-to guy, the head foreman; and they continually rotated him through all their construction sites. Rarely did he work in their headquarters or was confined to a desk job like Bridget. He liked hanging out and he enjoyed the activity at the sites filled with male comradery. The most accommodating part was the flexible hours. He could come and go as he pleased and there was nobody there to nag every second of every day. Freedom. The only drawback was his salary. He made nothing compared to his wife. His salary would never afford him the sleek car he drove, the boat, the jet skis, or any of the toys he was unwilling to give up. He had become used to what money could buy; and no matter the price—he didn't want things to change.

Not so with Bridget. Her job, as a high-powered attorney, was a pressure pot of stress and it was sucking the life out of her family time. She hated the demands and would have loved to find something more low-profile, but that was not going to happen any time soon. Her decadent salary allowed her family to live in a million-dollar home, along with all of Chase's toys.

Bridget straightened her skirt and tucked in her crisply ironed blouse. She put on her matching suit jacket and walked back into the kitchen. The boys were sitting at the table scarfing down their microwaved sausage and egg muffins.

Bridget poured herself a cup of coffee, walked over to the table, and sat down on a chair. She smiled at her hungry sons. "Okay, everyone knows what their responsibilities are today, right?" The boys nodded their heads. "Bryan, I hope you brushed your teeth this morning. You have a dentist appointment this afternoon, and you wouldn't want Dr. Ziff to reprimand you again. And Josh...make sure you put your baseball gear in dad's car. He'll be dropping you off at practice."

Chase was leaning on the kitchen counter sipping his coffee. His voice dripping sarcasm, he smiled and asked, "When do you think you will be home tonight?"

Bridget shrugged her shoulders, but didn't reply. She knew if she did, it would be the opener for another large fight. She always loathed when Chase started a fight in front of the boys. After a moment, she rolled her eyes and said, "I'll call you midday. Seeing as you never answer your phone anymore, I'll end up leaving you a text message."

Chase inhaled a deep breath. She knew how to push his buttons. He exhaled and said, "How many times do I have to tell you that I have people around me all the time? I'm usually at a site in a meeting. Now, how do you think that looks when my wife calls all the time?" He slowly shook his head. "Dammit, do you think I play all day?" Chase knew exactly the buttons to push, too.

Bridget ignored the comment and went to pour herself another cup of coffee. As she was leaning against the counter across from Chase she was thinking about how complicated life had become. It was much easier when they didn't have children and her job had not consumed so much of her time. They used to be happy, carefree, had actually liked each other. Now...rarely did they spend time alone, do things together, or have any form of intimacy—inside or outside of bed. Her life had become flooded with tremendous expectations and desperately meaningless, except for her sons whom she loved dearly.

"Do you think maybe we can book a vacation in the near future? I really need a break," she said out loud.

Chase walked over to the sink and dumped his remaining coffee out. "I have a trip planned with Boozer and Glen. I think Glen is making the plans. We were going to go to Mexico. We all need to let off some steam and wanted to do some deep-sea fishing. We didn't think the wives would want to go there. Is that okay...?"

"Would it really matter what I said? It seems you enjoy spending time with your buddies more than with me. All I do is pay for the trips—"

Chase slammed his hands down on the counter. "You really don't want to go there. You can never leave work—we know that." Then he sneered. "Stop bringing up money."

Her condescending smile spoke volumes as she lifted her brows. "Truth hurts?"

He hissed back. "*Truth is* you don't have any friends to take a trip with. You've left them all behind. I, at least, still have my friends!"

The pain in Bridget's eyes was very evident. Steeling her shoulders, she looked at the boys who were so busy eating breakfast they were untethered by the sardonic words being flung back and forth. She noticed Josh was looking at them with sad eyes. She made it a point to make sure that they curbed their disagreements and conversations out of the reach of his ears. He was getting older than the others and was beginning to realize the complexity of life and his parent's relationship.

"Okay, guys. Two dollars to anyone who can put their dishes in the sink, get their stuff together, and have their seatbelts buckled by the time I get into the car."

Immediately, four bodies rushed to the sink and were out the kitchen door in a flash. Bridget looked at the dirty dishes in the sink and smiled. Today the housekeeper was going to clean and she didn't have to worry about anything except getting the kids to school on time and making sure she made it to her meeting. She went into the foyer and grabbed her purse and briefcase lying on to the long entry table next to an overlarge arrangement of soft gold and ecru dahlias.

She looked up and met Chase's eyes briefly. A line of tension still strained the muscles in his face as he offered a bit of neutral small talk. "Have a nice day. I'll see you later. What's the plan for dinner?"

"I don't know. I'll pick something up on the way home. The kids like 'the Colonel's' chicken. If I'm going to be late, then I'll have Lupe make dinner. There's lots of stuff in the refrigerator. I went shopping Saturday." She forced a mollifying smile. "Thanks for taking Josh and Bryan." What she really wanted to say was, *'Enjoy your fucking easy day...you asshole!'*

Bridget strode out to the car and the four boys were belted in. She smiled and handed Josh and Bryan each two dollars through their rolled-down window. They hooted in excitement. Then she said, "Jax and Dylan, your money is on your dresser at home. I didn't want you to lose it at school. Bryan and Josh can buy themselves a snack at break time—you guys can't, so I put an extra snack in your lunch bag."

Bridget did a mental countdown of all her needed tools for the day: iPad, laptop, phone, purse, makeup, and calendar. It was all there in her large briefcase, so she climbed into the minivan and buckled herself in. "Are we all ready for a great day?" she asked, with false enthusiasm.

The boys all nodded their heads.

The house was finally quiet and peaceful. The never-ending chaos always left Chase's nerves rattled. A smile of excitement spread across his face as he ran upstairs to change his clothes. Minutes later, he slipped into a nice pair of creased slacks and an ironed shirt. Unbridled satisfaction appeared on his face as he looked at himself in the mirror. He smoothed and arranged his hair that was always cut at his favorite Beverly Hills salon and smoothed away the few wrinkles in his name brand clothes.

Chase looked around the room and grinned. His home was his castle. It had six-thousand square feet and included a custom basketball court, an exotic pool, and a four-car garage. Everything that would make him happy.

Chase and Bridget had moved into their lavish home a few days after their wedding at the Four Seasons Hotel in Beverly Hills twelve years ago. Even with over five hundred guests, Bridget's parents had paid for every dime. A conglomerate of corporate heads of companies, dignitaries, entertainment moguls, and the firm's business associates and their personal friends had all been invited.

Chase and Bridget didn't have a say in any of the preparations. Everything was arranged by three wedding planners and Bridget's mother. The wedding had been a beautiful black-tie affair that had left Chase's family stunned and feeling very insecure and insignificant.

Chase's family had never seen such a large circus of attention-grabbing snobs, nor had they ever experienced rubbing elbows with a large group of condescending elitist. They were just simpleminded people who went through life one day at a time.

Chase's parents and immediate family were lower-middle class. They were hardworking people who never saved a dollar and never went on vacation—except for an occasional camping trip to the woods. Their whole life had been a struggle as they raised their children in apartments and lived on fast food. His father could never hold down a job for more than a year, constantly going from one to the next. With no education and no skills, his father was only able to land minimum wage sales positions at nearby stores. His mother had been with Walmart for over twenty years and brought home most of the needed income in the household.

Chase was a 'nobody' until he met Bridget. He was a blue-collar kid working in construction. One evening while sitting in a trendy nightclub with a group of friends, he met Bridget. At first, his attraction to her was minimal at best. She was far from the prettiest young woman in the room. But she wore her wealth on her sleeve and that was eye-catching enough to him.

After spending that evening dancing and socializing, he knew he had found a good catch; and before the night was over, Chase had asked for her phone number. He knew he couldn't keep up with her dating expectations, but he didn't care. He poured on his charm and won her heart.

Bridget opened the door to a whole new way of life. He fit in surprisingly well. Chase enjoyed the affluent choices that were laid on his table. He liked the country clubs, sport cars, fancy clothes, vacations, and unlimited money in his pocket to use as he pleased. His earlier years filled with monetary struggles were soon forgotten. His parents could barely recognize their son as he clawed his way up the social ladder.

George Wendell, Bridget's father, had achieved tremendous success with years of hard work. He and a partner established a new law firm right after college that eventually catered exclusively to the rich and famous. After years of long hours and the building of his successful law practice, he brought in his only child—Bridget Leigh Wendell. At the beginning, it wasn't easy for Bridget, because she was so young and inexperienced. The demand to learn was exhausted with long, tedious hours that left her depleted of any kind of social life. In spite of her father's influence, she still had to carry her own heavy workload and maintain the integrity of the firm. Eventually, Bridget built up her value. With the exception of the long hours and her time spent away from the family, it worked well for her. Her life, from the outside, looked perfect to others.

As their only child, Bridget's parents constantly doted on her from the time she was born. With the expectations of grandchildren, they had given Bridget and Chase the large down payment for their home. After months of applying for home loans, Bridget and Chase had to finally put the mortgage in her father's name. It wasn't until after they got married she had found out that Chase had horrible credit ratings. With many charged-off credit cards, loans, and car repossessions, he was what creditors called a 'deadbeat.' Bridget was angry, and her parents were appalled—but Chase didn't give a damn. That was something that he never worried about in his life. He was just a layman who didn't respect the responsibilities of his debts.

Chase didn't care at the time that the house was placed in her father's name. He was just overwhelmed that they were getting their first home. But it seemed like lately, Chase had this need to refinance and put the house into both their names. Bridget had ignored his requests for a few years, but he continued pushing her. He knew, eventually, he would get his way, and for security reasons, he had decided it was a necessity. After all, it was their only asset and they did have a lot of equity built up in the large million-dollar home.

Chase slowly walked out of the closet and made a mental note to ask Bridget to get some loan documents from their bank so he could apply for a refinance. He had cleaned up his credit standings and he knew he would qualify. He walked into the bathroom and leaned into the mirror to ruffle his hair. He wanted that 'sexy' bed-head look. Chase was a very attractive man at the age of forty-five. A muscular six-foot frame, a dark tan, and a full head of brown hair made him look young.

Chase walked out of the bathroom and headed toward the stairs. Today was going to be a great day. He took out his cellphone and set the alarm to three o'clock. Having to be home by four changed his plans. *Damn it!* As he skipped down the stairs two at a time, thoughts of Christie set his blood to pumping. His eyes grew darker, the depths smoldering, and he rubbed through his pants in frustration to indulge his growing need for a release. He picked up his wallet and his keys on the small table and walked out the door. Instead of an after-dinner snack, he'd take her for brunch at the beach and then to a nearby hotel for a few hours of peace and quiet—lovemaking. He wanted her to himself.

Chase drove up to his destination and shut off the revving engine. The music continued to flow through his new Tesla Roadster. He leaned his head back and inhaled and exhaled with excitement as the country song ended. With one fast movement of his arm, with shaking fingers, he opened the door and stepped out of the car. He was feeling pretty brazen today. He had never come here in broad daylight, nor had he ever wanted her nosy neighbors to see him. That was all he needed to bring his world crashing down—one lousy neighbor that would tell Christie's husband about a strange man parking in front of their house. He knew it would absolutely destroy Bridget and the boys—but he didn't care anymore. Remorse wasn't in his vocabulary these days.

Chase took his cellphone and dialed her number.

"Hello," she answered.

He stood in front of the closed door. "Hey, you...what are you up to this morning?" he asked.

"I'm heading into work. When will you be there? Meet me in the parking lot for a little snuggling...." Christie's voice dropped down to a low, sexy mumble. "We could drive around the block and steal a quickie."

Chase smiled and whispered, "Oh, I don't know. What if we get caught? After all, I think a few people at work already suspect I'm into you. I bet they will all be sitting at their windows looking through their binoculars!" He began to laugh.

"Okay...." The sound of the disappointment in her voice was egging on his arousal.

"Look out the window of your front door."

"What...?" She sounded confused.

He laughed again. "Surprise! I'm at your front door, baby!"

Within a few seconds, Christie was laughing hysterically as the door opened and she catapulted herself into his open arms. With her feet off the ground, he spun around in circles over and over again. Her laughter was enticing and her hands around his neck pulled him deeper into a kiss that was filled with eagerness and the promise of good things to come.

She broke their kiss apart and whispered, "Why are you here? Let's go in the house before we're busted by my neighbors."

With her still securely nuzzled in his arms, he dragged himself across the threshold and laughed. "I'm taking you on a surprise trip. The next eight hours are going to be something you will never forget. Trust me." He placed her hand on his straining crotch.

Her eyes opened wide. "How can I trust you when I can't trust myself when I'm around you?"

"Come on, call in sick and let's go. The train takes off in twenty minutes and we have just enough time to get there!"

"Train...are you serious? We're taking a train?"

Chase bent down and gave her a slow, encouraging kiss. "Hummm.... You feel good. In a few hours, you're going to feel fucking amazing!"

Within fifteen minutes, they pulled up to the commuter train station and parked the car. He bought the tickets to go down south to their favorite beach. They both sat down on a bench and cuddled up next to each other.

People had gathered and were milling around waiting for the train that was due in a few minutes. He loved this commuter train and on occasion he would take Josh and Bryan to the beach for the day just to get away from the chaos in the house with the younger boys.

Chase looked at the beautiful, petite woman sitting next to him and couldn't stop thinking about how lucky he was. She was a perfect ten. Her light Hispanic skin color only added to her striking features, showing off her flawless face and big brown eyes. Her tiny waist and breast augmentation gave her the look of an exotic dancer. He could not get enough of her since their affair had started, months ago. Although their friendship had started out as a boss and secretary, from the moment he put his hands on her, he could not break his obsession. A few moments a day behind a closed door did not seem to satisfy him—his need only grew. Their trip to Las Vegas for her twenty-sixth birthday a few months ago had just been the beginning.

Chase knew he could lose everything if he ever got caught. He had been thinking about it more and more lately. When he wasn't with Christie, he felt like he was barely balancing on a tightrope of disaster. This daytime getaway was just what he needed to ease his frustration of his failing marriage and the pressure of his four sons.

"Are you ready to go play?" he whispered into her ear.

"Yes." She placed her hand on his thigh and smiled, looking up at him.

# CHAPTER 2

## Karyn

Why was it so hard for her to move her legs this morning?

"Please, God, don't let this be a relapse. I've been so good for the past few years without having to deal with any setbacks," Karyn mumbled out loud while she was lying in bed. Her legs felt like dead weight and the tingling was starting to sting the bottom of her feet. She didn't want to get up, but she knew she had to. With one child who had to go to school, she forced her legs to the side of the bed and gradually sat up. Once she was seated, she inhaled a deep breath and let it out slowly. *Why is life so hard? Or is it just mine?* she silently asked. Another of her many questions that really didn't have an answer.

Karyn pushed her fingers through her shoulder-length, wavy brown hair, trying to get it out of her eyes. She was not considered beautiful by today's standards, but she had the prettiest smile and brilliant green eyes.

17

Taking another deep breath, she slipped her feet into her well-worn slippers and sluggishly stood up. Karyn yelped in agony as the nerves in her foot reacted. With shooting pain that started at her toes and skyrocketed up her leg, she knew if she sat back down it would be a while before she got up again. So, with a sliding-type motion, she dragged each foot slowly forward and found her way into the kitchen to put on some hot water for tea. She loved to have her tea in the morning. Hot tea and a piece of toast with butter and honey on it was her ultimate morning pleasure. This was how she started the beginning of each week day, just before she would go into Penny's room and wake her up.

Penny was her eleven-year-old daughter who could not have been a more flawless child. She was the perfect pregnancy and a quick and easy birth. She wasn't a crier or a difficult child, and Karyn deeply appreciated that. After her first pregnancy with Kane, she had been afraid to have another child. She had been sick and miserable from the beginning until the end, and everything that could go wrong—did go wrong. As a baby, he was difficult. Allergies to formula, asthma, and colic were just a few of the things that made her life difficult and not really wanting any more children. She tried hard to forget those troubled years, but it was like a bad dream that always seemed to chase her.

Everything was different with Penny. She was the apple of her mother's eye and a tremendous support when it came to helping Karyn during the past few years. Especially now since Karyn's life-changing medical diagnosis. Their financial struggles had been hard enough to balance. With the additional pressure of Karyn's illness, her husband,

Jake, walked out. Not that his presence had really helped, but it left Karyn with multiple sclerosis, two kids, and a whole lot of bills to deal with on her own.

Sick or not sick, Karyn had to get up every morning and make her way to downtown Los Angeles. She worked 'under the table' for a small start-up company as a secretary, but she was only paid minimum wage. Her wages, along with a small disability check, barely got them by. If it wasn't for the help of a few government programs, she'd be on the streets.

Jake wasn't abusive—he was just downright lazy and an alcoholic. As long as he had enough money to fund his addiction, he was satisfied. He didn't like to work. He definitely could not hold down a job for more than a few months. He was just like his father, a man without ambition, an alcoholic who laid on the couch all day in a drunken stupor. Naturally, Jake's father had left his mother with five children to fend for. It was history repeating itself; and yet, Jake hadn't felt any guilt or shame that morning as he walked out the door with his suitcase.

Why Karyn had not seen this coming was a foolish regret she was now living with. What had she seen in him at seventeen? They were high school sweethearts who never understood or experienced a normal family life or a normal relationship, for that matter. Their life skills were limited. Education was never important and they had dropped out of high school in their senior year. Jake was immature and lazy then—and at thirty-three, nothing had changed. Only now, she was carrying the heavy burden of raising the kids on her own, without any help.

Karyn was working fifty-five hour weeks while struggling with multiple sclerosis and

19

the exhausting symptoms that went with such a debilitating disease. After a while, she had started to resent Jake's inability to support his children. For the first few years she begged him for help. Eventually she just gave up. She couldn't afford an attorney and the state had put her on a long list with other women that were dealing with deadbeat dads.

It had been four years since Jake left and he had not contacted or come back to visit his kids at all—not once. He never offered child support and never held down a job long enough for the government to force any child support from him.

An emptiness was festering deep inside her son, Kane. He was a very angry young man who resented his father for not visiting—though Penny couldn't care less. She was only six when he had left, and he had never formed any kind of connection with his daughter during that short time. Kane, on the other hand, had followed Jake around like a lost puppy. He loved his father to the point of distraction. He always begged for attention and never received more than an occasional pat on the head. Or kick in the ass.

As each year passed and Kane got older, his anger began to play out in a self-destructive way. He began to lash out at anyone who got in his way or challenged him—including his mother. Nothing scared him. He was bent on absorbing his father's sins. His father had left him a legacy of distrust and cynicism. Kane was now on a course of self-destruction and nothing Karyn could do or say changed it.

The neighborhood police officers knew well who he was; many times he had been taken down to the station exhibiting unleashed violence. School fights, stealing, bullying, and burglary were just a few of the list of infractions listed on his building criminal record. It was almost like he was challenging them to do something drastic to keep him from hurting himself. No matter how many times his mother went down to get him out of trouble, he wound up finding his way back in. It was a vicious circle and Karyn was at her breaking point. With no money to fight, flair-ups from her MS due to stress, and the pressing fear she would lose her job, she had lost control of her fourteen-year-old son. This had broken her heart and left her feeling inept as his mother.

Karyn loved her son. She didn't want him to end up permanently in juvenile hall or jail. CPS (child protective services) had entered into the picture when he was twelve, but nobody could stop or manage his out-of-control behavior. The year before, they had taken him out of Karyn's home for a month and placed him into the foster care system. CPS thought it might be a wake-up call for him to stop his rebellious attitude. All it did was intensify his resentment.

When he came back home, his escalating rage pushed him into more violent episodes of anger. His frustrated social worker had placed him in intensive therapy—but nothing seemed to work. No matter how hard and how desperately Karyn worked to change his defiant demeanor, nothing seemed to get him off that fast track to a disastrous future. He needed that strong male role-model he never had. He was eventually taken out of her home again and placed in juvenile hall with more young boys just like himself.

Karyn sat down on the kitchen chair. She still had a few moments left before she went in to wake up her daughter for school. Penny was a godsend; she helped when she could and tried her best not to create any more turmoil for her mother. Penny didn't want to see her mother have a relapse or setback. So, she helped out as much as she could to try to make her mother's life easier and less stressful.

Karyn took the last sip of her tea and slowly stood up. Her legs were trembling, but having those symptoms many times before, she took her time and began to carefully walk toward her daughter's bedroom. She didn't have to go far; the place they were living in was not very big. Two bedrooms, a compact kitchen, a small living room, and a bathroom were all condensed into an old single-wide trailer. Karyn called it a mobile home, because the truth was hard to deal with. Located in a rundown trailer park where many of the trailers were prefabricated structures, well over fifty years old, and lacked any kind of kindness on the eyes.

Over the years, with more government regulations restricting trailer parks, these parks were becoming scarce and held much less appeal than apartments and more stabilized living quarters. Unfortunately, this was the best Karyn could do to keep a roof over her children's heads. They were lucky for what they had, though. Karyn knew how much worse her situation could be.

Karyn walked into the dark room and immediately went to the window. She pushed the old curtain open to let in the morning sunlight. She turned and looked at her sleeping daughter and smiled. She bent over her daughter and almost lost her balance. Steadying herself with her arms, she tried once again and this time she gave her daughter a kiss on the cheek. "Get up, baby. You have school today and I have to work. Looks like it's going to be a beautiful day.

The sun is bright and I could see all the birds in the trees."

Penny turned over and lifted her hand up to touch her mother's cheek. "Gee, Mom, do I have to go to school today? Can't I play hooky; just today?" she pleaded, with a sweet look on her face.

Karyn put her hand on top of her daughter's and then brought it to her mouth for a kiss. "Not today, baby. You know they are watching us to make sure I don't neglect my parenting skills and allow you to destroy your attendance record. They would love nothing better than to find fault and take you away, too."

Penny stuck out her bottom lip and pretended to pout. "Damn, I thought maybe we could play hooky and go to the movies or something."

Karyn sat down on her bed before she lost her balance again. "Tell you what...."

Penny sat up and opened her eyes wide, hoping for a nod.

"This weekend we will go see the new version of *Cinderella*. I heard it is killer! Besides, I know what it's like to be the ugly and forgotten stepsister." Karyn smoothed the hair off her daughter's face and waited for her answer.

Penny smiled. "I'd like to see that movie. I heard it was awesome! Could I ask Brook to come? Her parents are always taking me places. Besides, Brook and I wanted to see that together."

Karyn nodded her head. "Of course! Maybe I'll drop you off in front and wait next door in the restaurant. That way you girls can laugh and have a fun time without me tagging along."

"We don't mind if you tag along, Mom. Brook really likes you. She said you're the best ever!"

"Let's talk about this later. Right now, you have to get ready for school. Maybe we will stop at McDonald's and pick you up a muffin for breakfast. That's only if we hurry!" Karyn tickled her daughter along her rib cage and they both began to giggle.

Within seconds, Penny was running toward the bathroom. Karyn stood up and walked toward the window. She glanced outside and smiled at the beautiful California morning, then closed the curtain as a shiver ran down her spine. She never felt quite comfortable in the dingy trailer park she resided. Sometimes the hairs on her neck would rise just thinking about that double murder a few years back. They never did catch the perpetrator and that had left Karyn always feeling uneasy. It had literally knocked down all her trust for humanity and left her locking the doors and windows and making sure all the curtains were closed tight. Those were scary times, and after that had taken place, nobody in the park felt safe—not even the children. With nowhere else she could afford in the area, she just prayed it was a targeted act of violence and not random.

Karyn walked into her room and began to get ready for work. As she picked out her clothes, she could hear Penny singing in the shower. With her clothes in her hands, Karyn sat down on her bed and thought about her childhood. She didn't remember what it was like to be young and carefree at eleven. She couldn't remember ever singing in the shower or giggling with her mother. Her childhood was far from happy. Abandoned at birth, she was left at the mercy of the courts and foster care system. She knew what it felt like to be alone and know that she didn't belong. She herself had traveled through the foster care system for six years without a permanent home, until the day she was adopted by a family with two young children. Even at such a young age, she had already been through enough to last her a lifetime. But suddenly, she was thrown into a whirlwind of dysfunction that left her emotionally depleted and psychologically damaged by her junior year. The system had released her to a family that could not deal with its own problems. Her new brother and sister were cruel and resentful and made her feel like an outcast. The parents tried so hard to make the transition work, but nothing they did worked. Years later, leaving with Jake had seemed like the answer to her problems.

She never wanted her own children to be put through that kind of childhood. She wanted better and happier, and so much more than she had ever had. Yet, life wasn't fair and she was trying the best she could to keep them all together. If only Kane could see or understand that—but he didn't.

Penny pranced into the room and looked at the regretful look on her mother's face. "Mom...how come you're not dressed?" She moved closer and gave her mother a pouty lip. "Why do you look so sad? What happened?"

Karyn looked at her daughter and tried to smile. "Just thinking about how much I miss your brother. I have a court date in two weeks. I'm hoping the judge will let him come home. I did everything they asked, including taking those classes every Thursday night. I keep crossing my fingers. I hope if they do release him that he will have learned his lesson and miraculously be a good boy again."

"He will, Mom. You wait and see!" Penny started tugging on her mother's clothes and said, "You better hurry. I'm only giving you ten minutes to get ready! I want McDonald's!" She started to giggle as she pranced back out of the room.

With a more energetic push, Karyn began to pull herself back together and released the negativity she had been carrying around all morning. She wanted just one break from all the dead weight she had been carrying around for the past few years. And as she had learned over the years, life didn't stop because she was feeling sorry for herself—it never did.

Karyn closed the trailer door and made sure it was securely locked. Then she ruffled her daughter's hair and said, "I think we might have a few minutes for those muffins I promised!'

Penny straightened down her hair and grimaced. "Oh man, you messed it all up!"

Karyn stretched her hand out and carefully put her hair back into place. "There.... Sorry, kiddo, I was just playing with you, and I forgot how crazy you get over making sure every hair is in place."

"Oh, Mom, it takes me ten minutes to get it right. With the gel and hairspray, by the time I get to school, it's always a mess and the kids tease me." Karyn looked at her pretty daughter. Penny's thin body was just beginning to blossom into a more womanly figure and her long, curly auburn hair, although unruly, was what most young girls would dream of. Her alabaster skin was almost flawless and not sprinkled with acne like most young girls her age. Big blue eyes showed her moods easily.

Penny looked into the trailer window to see if it would work as a mirror, then she began to straighten up her wispy bangs.

Karyn spun Penny around. "What do you mean, they tease you? Are you being bullied at school?" Karyn's face displayed a great deal of concern. "Who's teasing you? Is this something I should know about? Did you tell the teachers?"

Penny yelped at the top of her lungs. "Mom, stop it! Don't get crazy! Nobody is bullying me. Brook just teases me, because she has perfectly straight hair that always looks great. But when she laughs at mine, I mess hers up!" Penny started to laugh like a normal eleven year old would do.

They started to walk down the driveway and toward the exit of the park. Karyn didn't have a car. She couldn't afford one. Not just the price of the car, but all the expenses that went with it—insurance, gas, repairs, and parking. Where she worked downtown, parking could cost almost half of what she earned. She didn't know how people could afford those outrageous parking fees or the yearly insurance costs. Recently, gas had become so expensive a lot of people had stopped driving and started using public transportation. She didn't mind the walk and it gave her some quality time with Penny during those few blocks. Thankfully, Brook's mom had to pass their park every afternoon. She gladly took Penny home and made sure she got safely inside.

Luckily, they only lived four blocks from Penny's school and another block to the commuter station. She lived in a perfect location with easy access to everything she needed. It was just a shame that trailer park had made her a little uncomfortable lately.

They stopped off at McDonald's and got their typical Egg McMuffin. Penny loved to start her morning off with a special breakfast. They couldn't always, but it was a nice treat. And she always had a free hot lunch to enjoy thanks to her school. And on these special mornings with her mother, it was nice to sit down and watch the hustle and bustle of their busy McDonald's.

Karyn kissed Penny goodbye and gave her a big hug, whispering in her ear, "I love you, baby!"

"I love you too, Mommy!" Penny said with a grin.

"See you later. Be good and have fun today. You know how to get me if you need me." Karyn made it a point not to ruffle her daughter's head. She had been doing that for years as her form of endearment, but she made a note to stop.

Penny saw one of her friends and turned to run. "Bye, Mom."

Karyn began to walk as swiftly as she could out the door so she would not miss her commuter train.

Once down at the station, she could see it was going to be a packed train. It looked more crowded than normal. The space was filled with the regular commuters and quite a few others she didn't recognize. She turned her attention to a beautiful young woman reading a bridal magazine. She had never seen her before. Karyn sat down and felt a shooting pain run up her legs. She began or rub her calves, trying to keep the pain at bay.

# CHAPTER 3

## Harper

Harper dragged her arm out of the covers and shut off the alarm. She rolled over on her back and her fingers touched the warm muscled body next to her. She smiled and laid there for a moment, just listening to his baby snores and staring at his face. With each breath he took, she felt a tingle in her heart. Slowly, she inched closer to his body until her face came close to his and their bodies were touching. Her breathing began to escalate as her nose inhaled the scent of his masculine body.

She whispered, "Hey, you, it's time to get up."

She placed her lips on his neck and gave him a soft kiss as her body nuzzled closer. Slowly, her hand began to slide around his waist as she pulled him slightly closer. Harper laughed silently as she heard a deep groan rumble inside his chest.

She placed her hand on his face and brought her lips to his and gave him a soft, slow kiss. "I know this last month has been hell, but just think about next weekend."

His big blue eyes were still closed as a small grin crossed his face. All of a sudden, in a split second, his strong muscular hands flipped her over in one motion, leaving him lying across her tight supple body. He swooped her up in his strong arms and began raining hot kisses down her neck. When he was just about to kiss her breasts, she placed both of her hands on either side of his face and forced his eyes up to look at her. She needed to stop him before they both lost control.

With a voice so unsteady she could barely pronounce her words, she said, "You remember our promise, right?"

He nodded his head and gave her one of his famous smirks. "That was a promise made out of duress." He laid his head of brown, curly hair solidly on her chest and a groan slowly crept up his throat. Disappointment caused another similar groan.

She wiggled her way out of his dead weight and sat up. She exhaled her breath and started to giggle. "No, I don't think so. We are going to have a whole lifetime ahead of us and I want next Saturday night to be really special. Come on, Austin. You promised. This is just as hard on me as it is for you. I can't think of anything more wonderful than to be making love first thing in the morning. But you promised...and in a week, I will definitely make it up to you."

He pulled her hand and placed it on his crotch. "Talking about hard...this is crazy...." His voice was edged with frustration.

Harper looked irritated at his comment and pulled away. Austin lunged and grabbed her and brought her back down in bed and held her tight against him. "I'm just teasing you, baby. I know how much this means to you. I want you to know it's really hard to not have you—right here and right now. But I think it will be worth the wait. Besides, we'll have a whole week in Hawaii to wake up next to each other."

Harper reached her hand up and tapped his nose with a finger. "Yes, we will. A whole week of honeymoon bliss!" With that, she pulled her legs over the side of the bed and said, "I'll go start a pot of coffee." She knew when to stop and knew if she didn't, that slight edge of anger and frustration would blow up into another small fight about her promise.

Austin groaned as he watched her petite, naked body walk toward the door. She was beautiful inside and out, along with a quick wit and brilliant mind. Her long dark hair hanging down her back and her big blue eyes were what attracted him to her that first night in the hospital. He thought she was perfect then, but that was just the beginning.

Austin had brought in a buddy of his to the hospital who had just gotten into a bar fight and needed stitches in his head. Some drunk patron had picked a fight with his friend because of his large size and intolerable attitude. When they entered the emergency room, his buddy was placed in Harper's care. The cut was bleeding profusely, and she was as cool as ice as she stitched him up.

"Hey, are you always this detached to your helpless patients?" he had asked, trying to get under her skin.

She glanced at him with narrowed eyes. "Detached? I guess you don't see how 'attached' I am to this needle and thread." She lifted the needle up to make her point.

He rolled his eyes. "I meant your attitude."

"Why is it that when a group of men are drinking together, their overzealous testosterone levels flow and it ends up in a bar room brawl that leaves them with battle wounds?"

Austin began to laugh. "I guess we get pulled into that 'mucho macho' game. Then we wind up in the hospital ogling the pretty nurses!"

"Really? He's paying with one hell of a deep cut. All this so that his good buddy can sit and 'ogle' emergency room nurses."

"That's right! This was a big setup. He gets the stitches, and I get to ogle!" Austin raised his eyebrows as his eyes traveled from the top of her head, right down to her white nurse's shoes.

Harper turned her attention back to the stitches and ignored him. By the time she was finished, she had flung enough barbs that both the young men had felt the sting of her sharp tongue. Within those few minutes, Austin was completely hooked like a big bass who had swallowed the worm. He refused to leave until she accepted a date with him. Harper was unimpressed and not interested and let him know it in just two words, 'get lost!' She loudly sighed as she walked down the hall, unaffected by his multiple displays of infatuation and cat whistles.

For days he stalked Harper at the hospital. He brought her flowers, apologies, poems; all with one thing on his mind—a chance for a date. He openly pursued her in front of everyone until she finally gave him her phone number—just so he would stop annoying her at work.

She knew, that day that she handed him her phone number, that her life would be a crazy roller coaster. And over the past few years their relationship had sparked and blossomed. Harper loved him with all her heart and Austin could not be happier.

Harper grabbed her white terry cloth robe off the hook on the back of the door and put it on. Then she slipped on her white fluffy slippers and she was off to the kitchen to make coffee. Still laying on his back in the bed, Austin ran his fingers through his hair to push it out of his eyes.

With a big smile, Austin said to himself, "Thank God it's only seven days away, otherwise this tree trunk is going to become petrified." He looked down at his erection and laughed as he laid there for a few more moments to let his body calm down. Then he got out of bed and slipped into the bathroom. His morning routine was about to begin. Austin was a creature of habit; and it had taken a long time to finally fit it into Harper's lifestyle. She was spontaneous and always walked on the edge of time constraints.

Austin Lewis was from a conservative family and grew up in a suburb outside of Chicago. Strict routines had kept his family from wandering off in all directions. His was a large family, with eight siblings, and yet his parents managed to keep everything under tight control. Peace and calm filled their house and most meals were practically wordless. Everyone had their chores and everyone was expected to do their part. There was always a special time and a place for every little thing and nothing was ever left out. He attributed that to his mother. She had a special list for everything and everybody. Lists were posted and every one of the siblings knew exactly who needed to do what, what needed to be done, and when it had to be completed.

His father was like the sergeant of arms and his mother the enforcer; and they prided themselves on running a tight ship. From an early age each child was taught to respect their family and to value each other. His parents never gave one child priority over another. William and Leona Lewis had done a great job and their rewards were eight very successful young adults.

Harper Puzzio was a completely different story. Not that Harper and her sister were not successful—they were. It's just Harper's family came from a more bipolar-end of the spectrum than Austin's. Their lifestyle was born of the continuous chaos that most large Italian families thrived on. Her parents welcomed a house filled with uproar—they were loose, laidback, and loud. There wasn't a time when their house wasn't bursting with guests and hungry strangers. They welcomed everyone who needed a hot meal and encouraged lively and diverse conversations.

Her parents, Camilla and Nico, were both from large families. Each of their families had known each other for generations and their great-grandparents had actually come through Stanton Island together during the great migration from Italy in the early 1900s. For years they had lived in New York, but when they realized that the land of opportunity was budding in the west, both families moved to California. Packing up what meager valuables they had, they took a train and planted their roots into a new part of the country, one which was very different than New York. They opened a small Italian deli in the heart of Los Angeles that is still well-known and run by the families.

Harper's grandparents live in the large house they bought when they originally moved out west, only now, they lived with all three generations. Her grandparents were now very old and feeble, and their real enjoyment was constantly doting on their two granddaughters—Harper and Hilary. Harper was the baby and Hilary was six years older than her. The sisters were so different in their philosophies in life and their lifestyles showed it. Harper used all her energy at work as an emergency room nurse, or you could find her down at the mission feeding the poor. On the other hand, Hilary was a corporate executive and was as hard as nails—a relentless opponent in the boardroom. The sisters shared a tight bond that could not be broken.

Harper loved her sister and was so proud of all her accomplishments. Hilary's friends were all strong, self-reliant women who thrived in the hard-core corporate environment. With skyrocketing stress levels and paychecks that matched, they were consultants who played the game well. To purge herself from the stress of their jobs, Hilary and her friends traveled the world. They were the new generation of independent women who didn't feel the need to settle down and raise a family. They ignored the previous generations who felt a woman's place was in the home. Instead, they integrated into the 'all about me' generation that lived a more vagabond lifestyle, filled with independence.

Harper and Hilary hadn't spent much time together the past few years, because they were both so busy, but the time they did spend together was quality. And now that Harper was getting married, they were constantly on the phone. Hilary could not be more excited for her sister's approaching nuptials. She felt relieved that Austin and Harper would have children to carry on the name and traditional legacy of their Italian heritage.

Hilary didn't want children, and the expectation of being the older daughter had put a lot of unnecessary pressure on her. Sometimes it became a source of major conflicts between her and her parents. They wanted lots of grandchildren. Hilary and her friends were not willing to sacrifice their careers.

Hilary lived in Los Angeles in one of those newly renovated high-rise complexes that were popping up all over. Developers were beginning to restore abandoned buildings and homeless encampments, making way for the growing population of urban dwellers. They were rebuilding parts of the city that had fallen apart, leaving the new generation to enjoy areas that were once untouchable and uninhabitable. Hilary loved being in the 'hub' of city life.

Harper was more conservative. She lived with her parents until she moved in with Austin. She was not a city girl. The traffic, noise, and lifestyle was overwhelming. She gravitated more toward family type suburbia. Houses neatly fit into small communities that actually raised their children with grass backyards. Austin loved that about her. She was plain and practical.

Harper was excited about her wedding and included Hilary in on all the plans and preparations. Six months ago when Harper asked her sister to be her maid of honor became a major turning point in Hilary's life. What she was about to tell her sister was something she had been hiding for years.

That evening the sisters made plans to meet for dinner. Hilary had brought her best friend, Toni. Harper had met Toni before—many times at many of the family functions and they always had fun together. Toni knew how to get Hilary to let loose and unwind. She was different than Hilary's friends. Even though Toni had a strong outer shell, there was a softness that always appeared when Hilary got too intense and needed to be reined in. Harper liked that quality and she liked Toni. On that summer evening, Harper and Austin had invited Hilary to dinner so she could pop the question—'will you be my maid of honor?'

While they were sitting at the table waiting for their drinks, Hilary was clasping Toni's hand and looking a little uncomfortable. Hilary took a deep breath and exhaled. "How are your plans coming? Six months is a long way off, but you know it will creep up quickly!"

Harper was a little concerned at her sister's edginess. She couldn't help but notice that her sister's voice was cracking and her fingers were fidgeting with the silverware. It was odd. Her sister never showed any signs of nerves or agitation. She was a straight shooter who said it like it was without holding anything back. Tonight was different.

Harper took a sip of her drink and smiled. Then she looked at Austin and said, "Our plans are going great. I just hope I don't become a 'bridezilla' the week before. Mom is helping and Nana is trying her best, too. I'm just so thankful Nana made it through the surgery so she could be there to enjoy our day!"

Hilary glanced at Toni and rolled her eyes and then looked back at her sister. There was a long pause and then Hilary inhaled a deep breath and said, "I have something I've been wanting to tell you for a very long time. I just didn't know what to say or how to say it. Tonight seems like the perfect time. Although it is close to your wedding, it's something I need to put out there."

Harper looked confused and leaned forward. "What can be so intense in your life that you look like somebody has just kicked your dog?" Harper grinned and squeezed Austin's hand under the table.

Hilary looked at Toni, and then at their clasped hands, and sighed. "You know how much I love you. You know how much you mean to me. You know I would never do anything to hurt you or disappoint you. You know—"

Harper had been holding her breath in anticipation of some sort of horrible news. Unexpectedly she dropped her tensed shoulders, let out her deep breath, and interrupted her sister. "I know…period!" There was a long silence as the sisters looked directly at each other. Neither blinked, nor flinched.

Hilary was not sure she understood what was meant by the three words Harper had just uttered.

Harper leaned over and kissed her sister's forehead. "I know you love Toni." She smiled. "Did you think I was blind these past few years? I don't know why you were so afraid to tell me or the family. It was always obvious; Mom and I were just waiting for you to come to us."

Hilary exhaled deeply and looked at her sister, love shining from her eyes. "I just didn't want you to be disappointed in my choices." Her eyes began to well up with tears.

Harper leaned over and put her hand on top of Hilary and Toni's clasped hands. "That is your choice...to be who you are." She looked directly at Toni. "You had no reason to hide or be ashamed of anything. We love you both."

Harper called their waitress over. "Could you bring me eight shots of tequila?"

The waitress smiled and said, "Sure."

Within minutes a tray was set in front of Harper. Austin picked up the shots and handed two to each person.

Harper stood up and walked around to her sister's chair and she gave her a big hug from behind. Then she moved over to Toni and did the same. She picked up one shot glass in her hand and held it toward them. "To life—*L'Chaim*, as one of my dear Jewish friends would say!" They clinked their shot glasses.

Hilary just looked at her sister as the tears began to spill onto her cheeks. For a strong woman, she looked very vulnerable at that moment. Harper had not seen her sister cry since she was a young girl. With a low voice that could barely be heard, Hilary whispered, "Thank you, sis. Your approval means the world to me. I just hope Mom and Dad feel the same way. It would devastate me if they didn't."

"They will be fine. Your choices are yours to make. You deserve happiness. If Toni is your choice—then that's that." She paused for a moment. "To my maid of honor, and I mean that literally! To my best friend, confidant, and only sister...may you find love and happiness with Toni as I have found with Austin."

Hilary picked up the second shot glass and everyone followed. She held her hand high in the air and said, "If I searched the world over, I could not find a more loving sister than you! *Buon viaggio!*" The look of love Harper had on her face as she smiled at her sister's words would be remembered for a lifetime.

"Yes, to a 'good journey' for both of us!"

Harper quickly snapped out of her memories when she heard the spray from the shower hit the glass door and Austin's enthusiastic voice as he began to sing. His voice was so off-key she thought she was going to die laughing. He must have heard her laughter as he began to sing much louder.

She was sitting at the table looking over her list of things to do to get ready for her wedding on Saturday. It had been a long and nerve-wracking endeavor, with her parents constantly interfering in the plans. Their requests and suggestions were flooding her phone messages constantly, and with the wedding only seven days away, Harper was beginning to panic. So many things to do with so many people coming—with more added to the list—daily.

Harper moaned. "Bless my parents. They invited half of Italy. I have to make another call to the caterer to add another twenty-five people." Harper jotted down a note on that piece of paper in capital letters: TELL MOM TO STOP INVITING PEOPLE.

Her mom wanted everyone there to witness her happiness. She wanted laughter, dancing, and shouts of joy. She was proud of her two daughters. For her, coming from such a large family and only producing two daughters had been a tough blow. After five miscarriages between the births of her two daughters, the doctors had finally stopped her life threatening need to produce more children. With that done, she had finally realized she needed to concentrate on their two beautiful daughters—not what could have been.

Harper sighed, picked up the phone, and dialed the caterer. With that done she could check a task off the enormous list she was holding. Next she dialed the mission downtown. Austin and Harper spent one night a month serving food to the homeless and the needy families with children that were barely surviving on one meal a day. They enjoyed donating their time together to charitable causes whenever they could. Harper collected canned goods once a month from her fellow employees to bring down to the mission. It was something she was very passionate about. She constantly wrote letters to the president criticizing the government for not taking care of their own while they use resources they have to help the poor in other countries. She worried when she saw small children living on the streets with their homeless parents. She was also a realist, and knew she alone could not change or fix a broken government that catered to the rich and overlooked the poor. But she continued to recruit her friends to donate what they could.

She waited for someone to answer the phone. "Hello, may I speak with Alex?"

"Sure, let me go get him."

Harper tapped her foot as she waited for Alex. After a few minutes, she was getting ready to hang up when she heard, "Hello, this is Alex. I'm so sorry, we were having a nasty flood in the bathroom. Seems one of our old pipes decided it was time to let go and open up!" He laughed. "Who am I talking with and what can I do for you?"

Harper cleared her throat. "Hey, Alex, this is Harper. You know Austin and I are getting married on Saturday. In fact, I'm hoping to see you there."

Alex chuckled. "I wouldn't miss it even if my favorite Mexican soccer team was in the World Cup!"

"Don't over exaggerate, Alex! If your favorite team was playing, you would be sitting in the front row screaming like a maniac!"

He laughed. "You're damn right I would!"

"Well, I'm giving you a heads-up. We are ordering enough food for an army at the wedding. Even if all of my parent's friends show up and eat three plates of food, we are going to have a lot of leftovers. I want to donate it to the mission so none of it goes to waste. They told me they would pack it in aluminum trays, so I was hoping a friend of ours could drop it off later in the evening or you might want to take it with you. I know it will feed at least thirty to forty people, if not more. It would make me so happy if we could feed them ourselves on this special night like we do on other nights, but we are leaving on our honeymoon. So, Alex, I'm placing this on your shoulders."

"What a charitable idea. We would appreciate anything you could pass our way...including bathroom pipes!" He started to laugh again. After a minute, he said, "May God bless you and Austin. And I'm truly excited about your nuptials."

"Thank you, see you Saturday." Harper hung up.

Her black pen put a line through another item on the list. When one thing was marked off another was added. Harper took a sip of her coffee that was now cold. She grimaced. She had such a busy day ahead of her and she couldn't be late to get to the commuter train. She was going downtown to pick up her wedding dress. She needed the final fitting and while she waited they would press it for Saturday. Usually she drove downtown, but today she thought she would save herself from the anxiety of the heavy traffic and having to drive around the block for an hour looking for a parking spot, especially since the train was just two blocks from the alterations shop.

The shower shut off and Harper was leaning on the table adding something on to the list when Austin came in and grabbed her from behind. He was only wrapped in a towel around his waist. His hair was dripping wet and so was his chest. He leaned over her and laughed, playfully squeezing her. "Aren't you going to get ready for work? It's so not like you to run late like this."

Harper turned in his arms and smiled. "I'm taking the morning off to take the commuter into the city to pick up my dress. I might have lunch with Hilary if she isn't too busy. If not, I will drop the dress off and go into work. I took the later shift today, so I could get some errands done; so don't expect me home until late. This whole week is going to be major crazy for me!"

"Is there anything I can do?"

Harper shook her head. "You've already been so helpful, baby. And your mother has been so great too!" She leaned in and wrapped her arms around his neck and kissed him on the lips. "I know you have a full day ahead of you with the students. Just make sure that you get the stuff you need to get done out of the way. Confirm the tuxes, call the travel agent, and also make sure you have the gifts for your groomsmen."

Austin sighed. "With finals finally finished, it's all over but for the crying over their grades I'm going to post this morning!

I know the day is going to bring a lot of unhappy campers. I'll keep in touch, providing I'm not bombarded with angry students. Final grades are always a rude awakening for some of these privileged kids."

Harper clicked her tongue and shook her head. "I didn't realize that teaching at a private college would be so tense."

Austin laughed. "When you pay thousands of dollars for tuition for each semester and your son or daughter is too busy partying, something has to give. Parents have high expectations, and when their students don't execute, they naturally blame it on the professors. That's a fact in my profession."

"Well, I wouldn't know from that. I had my nose to the grindstone and it didn't come up for years until I had my nursing degree." Harper giggled.

"That's not what I heard from Becky. I heard you were the party girl who was so damn bright she didn't have to study!" He tweaked her small nose.

Harper sighed. "Becky was just jealous of Cheryl and me. She struggled through school and we were all so excited when she finally graduated." Harper ran a finger down his cheek and said, "Do you think our kids will be smart?"

He took her fingers in his hand and brought them to his mouth with a kiss. "If I have a daughter who is half as smart and as damn beautiful as you, I will have to beat the boys off with large baseball bats! If I have a son, he's seriously going to have to kick some ass and play a mean game of soccer. I'm going to coach the hell out of him!"

Harper started laughing. "Oh brother, I'm going to have to keep a close eye on you.

We have a lot of compromising to do. I am not going to let you run a tight ship like your parents! But there is going to be some structure, unlike my parents. I guess we both learned from them, whether we want to admit it or not!"

Austin leaned over and looked at the clock on the microwave. "Oh shit...if I don't get my ass into gear, I'm going to have a lot of explaining to do to the students waiting at my locked door!" Before he could release her, Harper put her hands on his face and looked directly into his big brown eyes. "Austin Lewis, I want you to know that I love you with all my heart, and don't you ever in our lifetime forget that!"

Austin's face shown with love. "I promise I will never forget that, soon-to-be Mrs. Harper Lewis."

Harper squirmed a little in his arms, "I like the sound of that...."

He immediately released her and slapped her bottom. "If you don't move your ass, you're going to miss the train, because I will throw you down on this cold kitchen floor and show you just what to expect our honeymoon night!"

Harper turned around and pulled his towel off. Before she could twist it and slap his bare body, he ran into their bedroom and began getting ready for work. She was laughing as he streaked through the apartment.

Harper grabbed her purse. As she was getting ready to walk out the door she took a post-it note and wrote a message to Austin. Then she stuck it on the refrigerator. She walked out the door, made sure it was locked, and slipped into the driver's seat of her car. "Six more days," she whispered to herself as she pulled out of her driveway and headed to the train station.

Once she parked the car, she checked her cellphone and walked over to the landing to wait for the train. She took a seat on the bench across from a couple. The older man with the younger woman looked very much in love. The woman was sitting on his lap and her laughter could be heard around the terminal.

"Six more days..." Harper said to herself.

# CHAPTER 4

## José

José, Angel, and Diego were three Hispanic friends flipping coins against the wall. Angel was José's older brother, a gangbanger with a lot of scars and tattoos on his short, muscular body as proof. Diego was a lifetime buddy who wished he was as tough as Angel, but didn't have enough street savvy to be accepted by the hardened gang members. José was the youngest and smallest of the three men. His short, conservative hairstyle was a reflection of who he was on the inside. José was muscular and handsome and had all the girls chasing him in school. He was going to be the first high school graduate of his family and they were all bursting with pride at his accomplishments. Unlike his siblings, he had kept out of trouble his entire life. He wanted to make his mother proud of him and he wanted to succeed. Not with a gun in hand or a gang affiliation, but simply with an education. With one more month of high school left, his dreams of college seemed so near, yet so far away.

The loud noise in the background was a string of squad cars involved in another neighborhood wild car chase. Police and news station's helicopters were racing in all directions through the sky and causing a commotion that was hard not to notice or hear. Life seemed to always consist of disruptions that could wake up the dead. Ambulances, sirens, helicopters, and gun shots were always a continuous reminder that life was an endless struggle in the barrio. No one was safe, and looking over your shoulder was the only way to stay alive. Boredom was a generator of crimes and the hood was filled with violence at almost every corner.

Diego asked, "Hey, man, where are you going, *chico*? You got big plans tonight with some cheerleader?" Diego laughed so loud that José could hear it echo down the block. He loved to tease the kid and make him angry. It had become part of a cat and mouse showdown that constantly annoyed José.

Diego spit at the cement in front of him and smiled as the stain grew bigger and bigger. Still bored, he spit again, trying to hit the growing stain. When he missed, the slew of curse words that came out of his mouth was worse than a drunken sailor. Diego had ADHD, so standing or sitting in one place was impossible. He used a lot of energy doing nothing. Today it was spitting. Yesterday it was knocking out windows of a vacant building with stones.

The three friends were sitting on the cement steps leading to the rundown apartment building they hated to call their home. They had been friends and neighbors for years Diego liked hanging with the brothers, José and Angel, although he rarely got to anymore. They didn't always have the tolerance to hang with Diego for more than a few hours. His mouth always got him into big trouble. He never filtered the things he said, and he didn't care who he offended. Nobody in the hood liked Diego, or his obnoxious behavior.

Diego lived with an aunt who had three children of her own to raise. His father had been a gangbanger years ago and had been killed in a neighborhood shootout. His mother took off with a boyfriend and occasionally floated in and out of his life when she was sober or in town. He had no one except his father's sister, and she was always pimping herself out for drugs. For years, his life was without any supervision. Dropping out of high school left him with too much time to get into trouble. He had an arrest record that was filled with minor infractions of petty misdemeanors, but they were overlooked by the judicial system. With his list of friends dying and incarcerated, he was beginning to think about moving to New York. On the verge of doing some time in the penitentiary, leaving was starting to become his new reality.

"Let me rephrase that question again, so you might understand it. Are you going to shag some bitch tonight or rob a store?" Diego growled at José, and then suddenly burst into laughter.

José turned a bright shade of red. He wanted to kick Diego in his balls, but instead he ran his hand along his jacket pocket, feeling the impression of the hard steel barrel with his shaking fingertips. "I don't know what I'm doing. So lay off me, Diego!"

Angel was staring at his brother. "What do you mean, you don't know yet? What the fuck!"

Diego shook his head and laughed. "I thought for sure you would have a plan or a place picked out already, *hijo*? You had better think really hard about this and what you are doing with those big brains of yours! You didn't come up with a clean rap sheet by accident. You worked hard at keeping your nose pointed in the right direction. Don't blow it now!"

"I don't know what I'm going to do...." His hand kept running along the hard shaft of the gun. It was almost a nervous reaction to carrying the illegal piece of steel that had been stolen in a robbery by his brother, Angel, and handed down to him.

Angel stood up. "Don't do it, bro." He kicked a coke can into the street and they watched a speeding car run over it. Angel hissed out, "You really need to get this idea out of that crazy head of yours. You've not been in trouble before." Angel punched José in the shoulder and narrowed his eyes. "Mom will never forgive you. Besides, who will be here to take care of her? What about that college education you want?"

Angel took a step toward Diego. Every part of his body was pulled tight like a violin string. *"No me jodas!"* he said in a growl.

José backed away. "I need to do what I need to do, bro. I made some promises to myself and now I need to keep them."

Angel and José's older brother Pablo had been killed in a rival gang shootout four years earlier. Angel was willing to bite the bullet, but he wasn't willing to sit back and watch José walk the same dark path. Angel pointed his index finger inches from José's nose. "I've spent a lifetime trying to keep you from doing something you would regret. This is a stupid idea. You need to listen to me. I know what I'm talking about. You don't know what it's like to be incarcerated with a bunch of fucking animals who will pounce on you the first chance they get. I do and it ain't worth it. Take it from me, your bro. Why don't you go put that gun in the house? You'll never be able to pull it off. There isn't a street-smart bone in that scrawny body of yours!"

Diego grinned and stretched his legs out in front of him, flipping a coin high into the air and catching it on the way down. He looked directly at José and shook his head. "Your bro, Angel, is like the cat with nine lives. One of these days he's going to use them up and poof—he'll be gone. Yeah, man, just like Pablo and Creepster. If the cat tells you to put the gun away—do it! You'd get your ass kicked straight down to the devil. Trust me, *hijo!*"

José stared at Diego with narrowed eyes and compressed lips. "Creepster had to go, he was in everyone's business. Both gangs were looking for him. Dead in the street is a good place for a squealer!"

Angel nodded his head slowly and pursed his lips. "Yeah, but why do you think the boys really took him out? Do you think he might have been stepping on their toes with his mouth or did he steal from them?"

José turned his head from side to side slowly. "He was a snitch. That is what happens when you shoot off your mouth and take another brother down."

Angel turned and looked down the alleyway. "Look, you've kept your nose clean this long, why do you want to do something stupid like rob a drugstore? They ain't got what you need and they ain't going to give it to you just because you're packing a gun! What is that going to do other than get you in the slammer?"

Diego's eyes opened wide when he heard 'rob a drug store.' "You best listen to your bro. He's right, you ain't got what it takes!"

José was angry and had put a lot of thought into what he needed and how he was going to get it. He had tried all the legal channels to get his mother the medications she needed to survive, but nothing had happened and nobody cared. Agency after government agency had told him that his mother either needed to do this or that or she didn't qualify, but none of them had stepped forward and given her the chemotherapy medications. She was slowly dying of cancer and the government didn't care or didn't want to deal with her. He was tired of shuffling paperwork and listening to the bullshit they kept repeating. His mother needed help and she needed it now.

Maria Loretta Sanchez-Rodriguez was dying and she was barely in her forties. José and Angel's mother was so discouraged with the government that she had lost her will to live. She had been diagnosed with stage-three colon cancer nine months ago, and yet not one appointment had helped her get any closer to the treatments she needed. It had taken her eleven months of traveling from one clinic to the next until one doctor at the county hospital had finally written a prescription to get a colonoscopy. After the test was taken, the prognosis was sent in a letter telling her to contact the nearest clinic to help her find an oncologist immediately. With eight million uninsured people in California, it seemed impossible to get an appointment. José was frustrated dealing with the broken system. Maria, a hardworking citizen of the country, was fed up and offended with how she had been treated.

It was just Angel and Jose left to care for their mother. Their older brother, Pablo, had been killed in a rival gang shootout four years earlier. Now, Angel only had room for anger and spent many nights away from home, hanging with his gang members. In his short twenty-six years, he had six pages of infractions of the law: incarcerations and a multitude of pending cases that would determine his fate once and for all. Jail was inevitable and it was right around the corner.

Angel couldn't find a job, nor would anyone hire a felon. He had made mistakes in his life starting at an early age, but there was no forgiveness or second chances in a society that catered to the privileged. Angel carried a lot of regrets in his back pocket. He didn't want his only brother left, the only son of Maria Rodriguez likely to survive, wasting his life away in some lousy penitentiary. He wanted José to make something better of his life. He was a bright boy with a chance to get somewhere or be a contributing inspiration to his Mexican heritage. José had vital tools to work with—like a high school diploma and an SAT test that showed he was a near genius.

Angel walked over and put his arm around his brother's shoulder. "I don't want you doing something stupid. This is not who you are. You've worked hard in school and you're almost there. We'll find another way to get those meds. I promise." His knuckles grazed his brother's chin with affection. Then he grabbed him in a fierce bear hug.

José pushed him back. "When? After she's dead? After our society has thrown her to the curb like a piece of shit!" With tears in his eyes, he continued to yell. "She's worked too hard at shoveling shit in this city to be treated like a piece herself! How many years did she work in the school cafeteria making sure the children had healthy lunches? Twenty years? She never complained. In fact, she never said a word, never was late, and never took a damn sick day! What did they do? Those assholes fucking laid her off." He shook with barely controlled rage. Rage that was eating him from the inside out. *"Why?"* he screamed. He paused and then whispered, "Because she got cancer, they discarded her as quickly as I can snap my fingers together." He held his fingers up high in front of his brother's face and snapped his fingers.

Angel grabbed José by the collar with narrowed eyes. "Yeah, that is what happens to those who work hard all their lives and still have nothing. But I am begging you, do not do it. It will destroy her. You are the only thing she has to hold on to. If something happens to you...."

José laughed, sarcasm lacing his chuckle with ice. "And you want me to be a good little boy, keep my nose clean and out of trouble, so I can be treated the same? Or maybe I can just sit next to her bed quietly and watch her cough up a fountain of blood?" He put his hand near the barrel of the gun and narrowed his eyes in anger. "I will do...what I need to do."

Diego shook his head. "Man, I don't know, José. You had better think about it. Listen to your bro. There are NO second chances."

José started to pace like a caged animal. "She has no second chance and no one who cares. When they laid her off, not only did they take her medical insurance, they took her dignity. The free clinic here doesn't work

with cancer patients. I have a list of meds."
He took the list out of his pocket and waved
it in the air. "If I go into a pharmacy, do you
think they will just hand everything over to
me?"

Diego said, "Nah, man. Not unless
they're staring down the barrel of a gun!"

Angel kicked Diego hard in the upper
thigh. "Diego, get the fuck out of here. Now!
Don't be giving my little brother any
support for his crazy schemes. The police
would rather shoot us on the spot and not
have to worry about crowding their courts
and jails. We see it all the time on television.
I don't want to see my brother lying on his
stomach with his back blown apart. Get the
fuck out of here!"

Diego picked up his paper bag that
concealed a beer bottle and started to walk
away. He looked at José as he shook his head.
"Okay, I'll catch you later...."

Angel yelled, "*Que te jolle un pez!*" He
glared at Diego's retreating back and then
approached José again. "I know you are
strapped—give me the deuce. I gave it to you
so you could protect yourself. I didn't give it
to you so you wind up in the slammer. Give
it to me!" he demanded.

José backed up a little. "No! I'm not
going to do anything stupid."

Angel took another step closer, his hand
stretching out further. "Place it here, punk!"

José bolted down the street. He yelled
over his shoulder, "I'll be home later. Tell
Mom I love her and to hang in there."

Angel yelled back, "Don't do it, *hijo!*"

José took off down the block as fast as
his legs would take him. He had been
deliberating over so much lately and today it
all come to a head. With his mother getting
sicker each day, he was under an unbearable

amount of strain and pressure. He had to do *something*. His head was spinning as he continued to jog down the street. After he had gained a few miles, he finally sat down on a bench in front of the train station. He took a few deep breaths, then he slowly got up and studied the schedule posted on the exterior wall. Maybe he just needed to take a ride to cool down his wild emotions. Glancing at the clock above the schedule, he noticed he had twenty minutes before the next train would stop at this terminal again. He spun around in all directions until he found what he was looking for. A large commercial drug store was across the street. He knew that if he could time it just right, he might be able to get those drugs from the pharmacist, jump onto the departing train, and hop off in the next town. *Can that be done? Can I avoid being caught? Would the timing be on my side?*

It had to...he had no feasible options left.

José stood in the ticket line behind a young woman with beautiful long brown hair. She was bouncing on her toes as she held out the money to the woman behind the glassed-in counter. She blurted out, "Can I have one ticket downtown? I'm going to pick up my wedding dress for this weekend. I'm so excited. Is the train running on time?"

The lady smiled. "To the very second. We are having a great day!" She handed her the ticket. "Congratulations, young lady."

José moved forward and handed the lady his money and didn't say anything. She smiled and handed him his ticket for the next train.

José sauntered across the street and walked through the automatic doors leading into the drugstore. He lifted up the hood from his sweatshirt over his head, blocking the view of most of his face. He looked around for the cameras and made sure he kept his face angled down. Calmly, he browsed down a few aisles. He was assessing the pharmacy department. There was only one customer at the counter, so he moved carefully toward the end of the aisle, waiting for the old man to leave. Preparing himself, he pulled out the list of prescriptions his mother needed. He was hoping it would give him enough courage to do this. When the man finally walked away, José observed the pharmacist behind the counter. He was a tall Hispanic man with dark wavy hair, big teeth, and a friendly smile. His head was down as he scribbled on a slip of paper.

Deciding to take the leap, José strolled up to the counter and smiled. "I need to pick up these meds for my mother," he said. His shaking hand held out the paper to the pharmacist.

After looking over the list, the pharmacist gave José a kind look and said, "I'm sorry, young man, but I need the doctor to call these in."

José clenched his hands on the counter. "My mother is dying and I need those meds. Can I please have them? I'll bring you more information later from her doctors."

The pharmacist shook his head and stared at the young man in front of him. "I'm sorry, son, but I have rules I have to follow." He was about to turn away when he heard the boy whisper something, so he turned back towards him again.

José got scared and for a split second he didn't know what to do. Filled with desperation, he held up his hand in the pocket of his jacket, showing the outline of the gun, and whispered, "I need those meds. Please get them or I will shoot you."

Compassion rather than fear reflected back at José from the pharmacist's eyes. "Don't do this. Put the gun away. This is not how you want to handle this, young man. Go through the legal means of getting these medications."

José's shaky voice grew louder as he began to wave the gun around. "I've tried for months. Our country won't help those in need, so I'm helping myself. Get me those medications now!"

The pharmacist turned to walk towards the back of the pharmacy when the gun accidentally went off. The sound of the gun ringing through the store terrified José. He froze for a second and then broke into a sprint towards the exit. Pulling his hood tight over his head, he ran as fast as he could. People were yelling throughout the store. .He had just committed a felony and this was going to change his life forever.

"Stop that man!" He could hear the voices screaming as he ran as fast as he could. His fingers trembling, his head spinning, he grasped his ticket tightly, his whole body in shock, and steered his racing steps towards the train that was just getting ready to close its doors. His outstretched arm stopped the door from closing completely and he took a flying leap onto the first step, just managing to board the train as it took off.

Jose's body was shaking as he began to relive the terrifying experience, over and over, in his head. Pulling his hood open enough to see through the window, José took one final look at the pharmacy. He could just make out hysterical customers running out of the front doors and the flashing lights of several squad cars as the train picked up more and more speed. Then his eye caught a lone man standing by the doors of the store.

It was the pharmacist. He was standing there staring at the train.

José's unsteady hand was resting on the muzzle of the gun inside his jacket pocket. His heart was racing a mile a minute. He didn't know what to do or what was going to happen to him.

He walked away from the door, over to the nearest seat, and sat down. He began to calculate what his next move was and what he was going to say or do if he got caught. He was certain of one thing—he needed to dump the gun. Remembering what his brother told him, he looked around the crowded space for a nook to hide the gun. Carefully hiding his actions, he slid out the gun, rubbed off all his prints, and tucked it into a deep corner of the seat. With a shudder, he leaned forward and rested his head against the seat in front of him as tears rushed down his cheeks in a sudden torrent.

The young woman with the long brown hair was sitting on the bench in front of him. She turned around and placed a soft hand on his shoulder. "Are you okay? Is there anything I can do?"

José never looked up.

# CHAPTER 5

## Yun

"Wake up, Yun!" Katy Blackwald yelled from across the room.

The alarm continued to buzz. This time Katy shrieked louder. "Yun! For god's sake, shut that fucking alarm OFF! I've got a bloody hangover and you're making it worse!"

There was still no answer and the alarm continued to buzz. Katy finally jumped out of bed and stormed over to the small bedside table and pounded the buttons on top of the alarm to stop the infernal buzzing. She exhaled in a huff when she realized the bed was empty and rolled her eyes as she slowly walked back to her warm bed and fell on top of the thick down comforter, rolling herself up in it. Katy was a beautiful girl with a slim body, a perfect light complexion, and model-like features. Her long blonde hair hung down her back as she curled up into her covers. With a big sigh, she closed her eyes and tried to get back to sleep.

Suddenly, the bedroom door opened and Yun ran into the room. She was trying to catch her breath from the two flights of stairs she had just flew up—taking two steps at a time. She glanced at her alarm and then at her roommate. With a very repentant face, she walked toward the big lump wrapped in the comforter and sat down on the edge of her bed.

Katy didn't move or even acknowledge the bed as it slightly bounced when Yun sat down. She continued to lay there perfectly still and silent. Her head and closed eyes barely could be seen sticking out of the blanket.

"I'm sorry, Katy. I meant to shut it off earlier when I went downstairs to tutor Lee. I guess I forgot." Yun waited for a response. She knew Katy wasn't asleep. She could tell by the way her chest heaved up and down and her closed eyes twitched.

Slowly Katy turned onto her side. She viewed her friend and quietly asked, "How do you exist on so little sleep? You went to bed way after me last night and now you're up before the crack of dawn—tutoring. You never let yourself have any kind of fun. Work and school are the only two dimensions in your life."

Yun smiled. "I wish I could explain. So many things push me harder and harder to get to where I'm going." Yun moved a little closer to her friend and tapped her hand. It was a gesture that Katy had gotten used to. It was a form of acceptance of their conversation. Yun crossed her legs Indian style as she got more comfortable. "We have been raised with different values, different lifestyles, and different cultures."

"Please don't give me the crap about your culture, skin color, or inherent lifestyles! I get so tired of hearing that on campus. That, to me, is a bunch of bullshit!"

Yun sat back against the wall and smiled at her dear friend. She was a petite Asian girl with flawless skin, a small nose, and beautiful full lips. Her jet black hair was cut shorter in the back and angled longer towards the front, a trendy cut that showed off her smile. She wasn't pretty, but the way she angled her head and opened her dark eyes was very endearing and gave life to her quiet personality.

Katy just laid there looking at her friend. "Different worlds? How so...? We were both raised in the United States since birth. We have both been exposed to the same things."

"I understand that, but our philosophies are different."

"We are young, adaptable, and that is a small part of who we are. I don't get why people still hide behind all kinds of miserable excuses!"

Yun sighed. This was going to be another long conversation. "We have been raised with different values, lifestyles, cultures, and financial backgrounds. You came from immense wealth. My parents gave me up to save my life. There was no thought of love or how I would feel living with strangers. It was purely done on a 'survival' necessity. It was her country that tore us apart."

"But you live here now..." Katy said.

Yun sighed again. For the past few years, this conversation had been a battle. "I was born to an immigrant Chinese family who spent every penny they had to fly my young mother here when she was pregnant so that the Chinese government would not put her second child to death. You were raised in wealth and swaddled in gold filigree baby blankets. There is the difference...."

"Yes, but that law was from 1979 and it was repealed a few years back, so now the younger generations don't have to go through that. It's the past, and look where you are now. You're one of the brightest young women I know. You're the top of your class and you have an enormous group of sorority friends who love and adore you. I guess what I'm trying to say is...why continue to punish yourself for something a government was responsible for over twenty years ago? Let it all go. Live for today."

No matter how many times they discussed it, Katy had no clue about certain issues, especially when culture was involved. Katy had a hard time grasping the fact that nothing was more important than family. Adopted children knew what Yun felt. They could identify with that feeling of being lost or forgotten. "You just don't get it, Katy. I'm twenty-one and when I was born it was traumatic for my parents. I can't even imagine what they went through so that I could live. You've never had to deal with a government tearing families apart, taking the lives of children, or forcing sterilization. You could never even begin to process what it's like to be alone, to not know a single thing about your mother and father aside from their names. I have a brother I've never met. How is that fair? I think about it all the time."

"You should be happy to have freedom from that oppression. Instead, it upsets you."

Yun nodded. "Yes, because I don't have a family. I wonder how your parents would have felt giving you up or your two brothers. I heard that my mother died years later of a broken heart. I have to become successful and earn enough money to pay back my aunt and bring my father and brother to the United

States. Don't you see, that is why I was brought here? I was their only hope or chance of ever leaving the oppression of the Chinese government. I was their one-in-a-million shot—and I am almost there!"

Katy leaned forward. "When will you have paid off the debt you feel you owe? Your aunt used you as a slave to cook and clean."

"Sometimes talking to you is like talking to a blank piece of paper. You were raised in generations of wealth. Enough wealth that you could pick and choose any school you wanted to go to and your parents readily paid for it. When did you ever have to work yourself to the bone, just to survive?" Yun sighed, again. "I have incurred a mountain of debt to give myself a prestigious education that might guarantee me a decent paying job. My aunt never paid a dime of my tuition. I worked in her restaurant, from a very early age, just to help her pay for the living expenses she incurred from keeping a roof over my head. I don't mind paying her. My parents and I owe her a big debt of gratitude."

"Gratitude? Are you kidding me!"

"She did not have to feed or clothe another mouth, she had four children of her own. She wasn't really even a close relative. She was a sister of a sister of my father's brother's best friend—a distant nobody who opened her door. I may never really be able to repay her, but I can make her and my family very proud of the child they saved."

"You've made the Dean's List every semester, you hold two jobs, not counting the tutoring you do on the side, and you manage on only three or four hours of sleep a night. Isn't that enough?"

"Not until I can send my father and brother a plane ticket with their visas."

"Well, you have a few more semesters to go, and then what are your plans?"

"Medical school. Who knows...maybe I will even go back to China to help my own people." Yun laughed, then she looked very meditative. "I want to go back and visit my father and brother. When my mother died a few years ago, it became one of my biggest regrets in life."

"How can that be a regret?"

Yun looked up with tears in her eyes. "They must have taken every *yuan* and *kuai* they earned for years to afford a trip to America—to go home empty handed."

"I guess it's just hard for me to comprehend." Katy was considered the black sheep of the family. She didn't want to attend Yale or Harvard like her family's past generations. She wasn't interested in impressing anyone with the status of her education. She really didn't want to go to college—period. Nor did she want to go into the family business. She wanted to open up a small bookstore with a little coffee and tea bar and serve homemade scones.

Her dream was shunned by her family; they thought it was a good joke. In order for her to have any kind of peace from their constant nagging over her education, she succumbed to a California college with an outstanding reputation, but nothing compared to their expectations. All she wanted to do was live her own life and patiently wait for her great-grandmother's trust account to mature so she would be able to open up that small bookstore.

Katy and Yun had become friends their freshman year in college. They didn't know anybody and were unfamiliar with the area that the college was located in. They each posted a message on the campus bulletin board—'looking for a roommate.' Five years later, they were inseparable and the best of friends. With their friendship came valuable lessons.

Katy had learned slowly over the years that all the adversities her friend had endured through her childhood had made her very strong. Living with Sunlee Yang and her family had been a mixed blessing. Although not many words had been spoken about her early childhood, there was always a sorrowful look that crossed Yun's face when she talked about her adopted family.

Yun didn't know very much about her parents or her brother. She only knew what Sunlee had carefully chosen to share. Occasionally, once a year, a letter would arrive addressed to Yun. Even that didn't lead to much information. Yun wanted to write back or try to make contact with her birth family, but Sunlee constantly discouraged her.

What little Yun had found out about her parents had left her very curious. The village her parents lived in was an area in which the poorest rural households derived a large share of their income from the small surrounding rice fields. Over the years, frequent natural disasters, especially floods and droughts had created deprivation for these pockets of small remote villages. Their lives in these isolated areas lacking paved roads, markets, and safe drinking water had limited their ability to communicate with the outside world.

Their lack of education had her mother and father walking miles to the nearest small community to find someone who could write a note to send to Yun. The notes contained very few words, but always contained a heart with an 'm' inside. What that meant was a mystery to Yun. She could only surmise that it meant they loved her. Sometimes she would pull out an old note she had hidden to remind her that there was a small family out there that loved her.

Katy jumped out of bed and stretched. Her beautiful features were more prominent when she pulled her long blonde hair up in a ponytail. Her rosy cheeks, blue eyes, and perky nose were handed down through the generations.

She sighed. "I guess I should thank you for waking me up or I would have slept the day away!"

Yun smiled. "I guess my alarm worked then? I, too, have a long day ahead of me. I promised Sunlee I would work in the restaurant."

Katy scowled. "I thought you weren't working there anymore."

Yun shrugged her shoulders and pursed her lips. "I'm not. Her son Cheech asked me as a favor. Sunlee is going in for some medical tests. She hasn't been feeling well and they want to do a scan." Yun shrugged her shoulders again. "What could I say?"

"You could say no!"

Yun took a deep breath before she answered. "I don't have a class until evening. Then I have two tutoring sessions meeting me here." Yun pushed her legs over the side of the bed and stood up. Her petite body was muscled from years of riding her bike everywhere she needed to go. A car was not a luxury she could afford. When she needed to go to Sunlee's restaurant down town, she either took the blue rail or the commuter Metrorail.

"Is she at least going to pay you?" Katy's upper lip curled in disdain. It was always

68

hard for her to hold back her dislike of Yun's adoptive parent.

Yun put her hands on her hips and pouted her lips. The broken gold coin necklace around her neck sparkled from the sun shining in the window. "I really don't know. I really don't care, Katy. I'm doing this for Cheech. I do have an allegiance to the family. I was raised with Cheech, Lu, and Bai. Cheech is a good friend of mine. He never asks for anything unless it's necessary. I imagine Lu and Bai will be going to the doctor with her. Honestly, I don't know where you get your condescending attitude towards Sunlee. You know, I'm really terrified there is something seriously wrong with her. Lu and Bai have mentioned she's coughed up blood a few times."

Katy looked concerned now. "Do you really think there is something wrong with her? I didn't mean to be so flippant, but she always seems to want something from you. Last week she needed you to pick up some produce and bring it down to the restaurant. The week before, she needed your help lifting up the planks and cleaning the floors in the restaurant. I mean, I could go on and on...."

Yun walked over and put her arm around Katy's shoulders and tweaked her nose. "Since her husband passed away a few years ago, everything has fallen on her shoulders. With Cheech, Lu, and Bai in college, she is alone more and more to handle the responsibilities in the restaurant. She's not that young anymore, and I feel a few minutes of my time is a big help to her. Come on, Katy! Don't be so hard on Sunlee. She has done the best she could with very little to work with. She has not had the best life. Her husband, Chin, wasn't the easiest man nor was he the hardest worker."

Katy hugged Yun and said, "You're a good person, my friend." She tapped Yun's nose; her nose was too small to tweak. "I can be a Debbie Downer sometimes! You know how to knock some sense into my little head!"

"I'll have a few minutes between coming home and tutoring. Let's go to our favorite hamburger stand tonight. I could use a burger and fries!"

"Great! As long as I can treat. You bought me dinner the last time!"

"Nǐ zhè tǎo yàn guǐ."

Katy pushed her friend away and started to laugh. "It's a good thing you made me take Chinese as my language elective!" They both started to giggle. "FYI, you're the 'pain in the ass!'"

Katy picked up her towel off a chair and left the room to take a shower. Yun stood there for a moment to think about their conversation. Life seemed like a never-ending rollercoaster of emotions. She knew she was lucky, she knew her life was better than most, but she also knew pain more deeply than anyone would ever guess.

Yun straightened up the apartment and put all her books in her backpack. She needed to get a move on if she was going to catch the train to Chinatown in downtown Los Angeles. She didn't feel like riding the ten miles on her bike.

Hefting her backpack up onto her shoulder, Yun headed for the door, but stopped at the chalkboard. She wrote a simple note to Katy:

> *See ya later, alligator. I can't wait for that big, juicy hamburger!*
> *Love ya, Y*

# CHAPTER 6

## Terrence

The alarm went off and a muscular arm jetted out from under the covers. He tapped the dresser until he found the cellphone that was making the loud, incessant noise. Terrence Martin opened one eye and pushed the 'off' button, sending the room back into blissful silence. Exhausted from his endless days on the baseball field, he laid back and his body began to relax. From the beginning of his day to the end of his evening, there was never a spare moment. He had everything precisely timed and his schedule was balanced like a tightly wound watch.

It was time to wake up and get started on the full day he had ahead of him. He laid there an extra minute to enjoy the peace and calm of the morning. Nothing would be quiet again until he crawled back into bed later that evening. He worked hard. One of his hands touched the snoring lump cuddled up next to him. Terrence smiled in the dark. The lump kicked and then settled, dreaming of what, he didn't know. Terrence's smile never left his face. Acknowledging his tight schedule, Terrence reached over to the dresser and turned on the light. With a grin, he swatted the lump, an effective trick for waking someone up.

"Owwww…that hurt!" the boy under the covers screeched.

"It was meant to. Now, don't get crazy and tell your teacher that your pops beat you within an inch of your life. That was just a wake-up tap!" His arms encircled the lump and he held on tight.

"Gawd, Dad! You're smothering me. Let go of me or you're going to be sorry!" Timothy yelled, his voice muffled by the covers pulled over his head.

"Yeah, what are you going to do about it…if I don't let go?" Trying to hold down his bucking son was like trying to hog-tie a pig in a pool of mud.

Timothy's arm came out of the covers and grabbed at his father's t-shirt. "I'm going to knock your block off! Let go!" His yells were sharply punctuated by short bursts of laughter.

All of a sudden, Terrence flipped onto his back and went still. Timothy immediately flew out of the covers and tackled him. Then they both began wrestling on the bed, laughing and screaming. Rolling around on the bed had become one of their morning rituals. It was also a fun way to get Timothy up before getting him ready for school.

"I got you, Dad!" Timothy shrieked as his fingers gripped the neck of his shirt and began to tug.

"No, you don't…. I have you now," Timothy said, gulping for air.

Terrence laid on top of his son, balancing his weight, with just enough force to contain all his energy, so that his son could calm down. Timothy was one of those kids that when he started something, he didn't want to stop. On occasion that would lead to someone getting hurt. Terrence had learned to curb the rough housing, but still let his son enjoy the playfulness of the game. Timothy didn't know anything else. His mother had left right after his birth. She didn't want the baby or the responsibility. To her it had just been a few nights of excitement with a good looking athlete. She was a baseball team groupie; she followed the teams around looking for any kind of attention.

Terrence had met Sophie while he was playing for the Angels. It was the first summer after he had been drafted by the team, just after his college graduation. Four years in high school playing soccer, football, and baseball had him on the radar of most major colleges. The constant letters and calls had his head spinning as they tracked his four years of high school, pushing him to play in the scout league. Eventually, he had to make a major decision that would follow him the rest of his life. Was he going to be drafted from high school and go straight to the minor leagues? Or was he going to forgo the draft and take a full scholarship to the college of his choice? When he had finally announced at the end of his senior year his choice, there were a lot of disappointed faces.

With a full scholarship to the best university in California, he made the commitment hoping it would give him enough time for a solid education before he considered the major leagues.

He was the star on his college team and drafted to the minor leagues in the third-round picks. Everyone thought he would go out higher on the draft, but they had a little reservation as to his arm. Occasionally, he was taken out of the lineup because of tendonitis. Not uncommon, but something that definitely put him on their radar.

The minor league was a rude awakening for him. He was no longer in the spotlight. He was just one number in a list of hundreds.

Everything was so new and strange to him. He had chosen a university close to home so that he could remain near his mother. After all, Vera Martin was the only person he had left in his life. There were no brothers or sisters, aunts or uncles—it was just him and his mother. His father had skipped town when his mother was pregnant and never returned. His mother devoted her life to working two jobs and raising him— giving him strong values.

Timothy worshipped his father and Terrence loved his son. But Terrence learned a hard lesson—he became cynical and distrustful of women. He played professional ball and took care of his son and mother, but stayed a mile away from all those groupies.

Timothy began to wiggle his way out of his dad's arms. "Let me go, Dad."

"Give me one reason why I should?" Terrence laughed.

"Because I can't be late for school. I have a big test today and if I'm late or absent, I will get a big 'F'!" He kept squirming around with all his might.

Terrence released his son. "Go get dressed and I will make breakfast. What do you want today—cereal or toast and bacon?" Terrence hopped off the bed and winced as a tremendous pain shot through his left knee and down his leg. His knee had been giving him a lot of problems for the past six months. He tried to hide it the best he could, but the slight limp and pain that crossed his face during workouts was a dead giveaway to those who knew him. He didn't want to complain to his coaches or the team doctors. He knew if they suspected anything was up, they would immediately place him onto the 'injured' list or even send him back down to the minors so they could bring up a youngster. Teams don't really care about the emotional rollercoaster of the players. Like everywhere else in life, winning was the bottom line—at any cost.

His contract only had two more years left. He had already been told they would not renew it and it was likely that no other teams would trade or pick him up. He was already a broken 'old' player. He had already worn out his welcome by a few years. Two years older than the average in the major leagues was almost like a lifetime for many of the players.

Terrence expected that eventually they would buy him out and send him packing. What he was going to do when that day came was beyond his comprehension. He did have his degree from college, but he had never joined the workforce to accumulate any experience.

Terrence was limping into the kitchen to make breakfast for Timothy when the phone began to ring. The loud noise startled him. Nobody ever called him this early in the morning. Unless it was his mother. He pulled out his phone, placed it on speaker, and said, "Hello."

The strong male voice on the other end blasted out, "Hey, kiddo. Pedro and I want you to come downtown to headquarters today. We have some things we need to discuss."

Terrence hated when his baseball managers called him 'kiddo.' He knew something was up and he had a sneaking suspicion it wasn't going to be good news. "What's up? What kind of powwow are we having? Do I need my agent?"

"Come on down. We just want to talk. You might want to take the commuter train and avoid the traffic so we can get back to the field for practice in time."

Terrence smiled. That was the biggest crock of crap he had heard in a while. Who did George think he was talking to—an idiot who would drink the Kool-Aid? Something was up.

He stood there for a moment and then decided he would call his agent and attorney on his way to the commuter train.

It was barely 7 a.m. and his mother would be home in an hour. She worked the graveyard shift at a local drycleaner. She had worked there for over twenty-five years. They allowed her to pick the evenings she needed which enabled her to watch Timothy when Terrence left town for away games.

Timothy walked into the kitchen and looked at his dad, who was staring at the wall. "Is everything okay, Dad? Who called this early? Is Nana okay?"

"Yeah, everything is fine. George and Pedro want me to take the train to meet them this morning. I guess they want to talk about my future."

Timothy got excited and jumped up and down like a typical ten-year-old. "I wish I could go. Can I go? I love taking the train!" His eyes lit up with excitement.

Terrence nudged his son to sit down while he buttered his toast. "I thought you had a big test today? You know that grades are important for your future."

Timothy looked disappointed. Terrence came over with a plate filled with toast and bacon and ruffled his hair. "Tell you what...."

Timothy suddenly perked up and gave his dad a big smile. "What?"

Terrence looked at his son and started to laugh. "You have my word. The next open weekend I have, we will take the train down to Olivera Street and hang out. Then we can have some Mexican food at your favorite place."

Timothy danced in his chair as he shoved most of the toast into his mouth in one bite. Without stopping to chew, he asked, "Promise?"

Terrence sipped his coffee and nodded his head. "Come on, let's get a move on. We both have a big day ahead of us."

The next hour was a rush, showers and getting dressed. When they were both done, they walked back into the kitchen, first Terrence and then Timothy.

Terrence narrowed his eyes at Timothy playfully. "Did you brush your teeth?"

Timothy let out a big sigh. "Yes, Dad."

Terrence smiled. He dug into his pocket and pulled out some cash. "Here's some lunch money. Don't spend it all on candy and crap! Buy something healthy for once!"

Timothy held out his hand as he rolled his eyes upward.

Terrence grabbed his son's backpack and was walking toward the door. It opened and his mother walked in, carrying groceries. Her steps were heavy and she looked older than her age. Terrence looked at his mother and felt this overwhelming shame of having to place the burden of his son in her tired hands. He wished things had been different and that he had thought more of the consequences before he unzipped his pants.

But then, life does come with mistakes that can't be corrected.

Terrence hurried toward his mother and took the two bags of groceries from her arms. "Why did you carry these heavy bags from the car? These are really too heavy for you. Gosh, Mother, you should have gotten Timothy or me to help. You just got off work and you must be exhausted."

Vera smiled. "I'm fine. I'll get some sleep later. I wanted to put up a pot of spaghetti sauce for the week."

"Ma, why don't you leave that for Emma? She's supposed to cook and clean. Isn't that what I'm paying her for?"

Vera smiled and shook her head as she unloaded the groceries. "She makes the most awful spaghetti sauce. The last time it was so bland! I'm fine. I'll get it started and then lay down. Don't you have to get going?"

Terrence shook his head and gave his mother a hug. "Love you, Mom."

Vera gathered Timothy into her outstretched arms. "You be good for your Nana and get good grades. Do you have a lunch?"

Timothy nodded his head and held up the dollar bills.

Vera opened a grocery bag and took out a big apple and a granola bar. "Here, put these in your backpack. You might need a snack."

Timothy held on to his grandmother and gave her another hug. "Love you, Nana."

She looked down into his face and smiled, her big teeth showing. "You do good in school, remember that, young man."

Timothy and Terrence walked out the door and got into his sporty Tesla. It was his pride and joy and he loved it much better than the Porsche he once had.

Once he pulled up in front of Timothy's school, he stopped the car. He looked at his son and said, "You got everything, buddy? You take the bus home, and if you can't make it, then give Nana a call and she'll come get you."

Timothy grabbed his backpack off the floor and opened his door. One of his buddies came running up and said, "Come on, hurry up. Jax and the guys are waiting for us."

Timothy hopped out of the car and was soon lost in the crowd of kids walking up the stairs and into the school. Since Timothy had forgotten to close his door, Terrence tried to lean across the car and catch the handle on the door to pull it closed. On the third try he winced in tremendous pain and began to rub his shoulder. It was his right arm and it had been giving him some trouble lately. He was worried that maybe the rotator cuff had a small tear. He sat there for a moment and rubbed his aching shoulder.

Catching him off-guard, a very calm voice, as smooth as glass, asked, "Is your shoulder okay? I noticed you gasped in pain. You really should see a doctor."

Terrence looked up and felt foolish for sitting there when there were cars lined up to drop off their children. "Yeah, I'm okay. I just had a slight pain in my shoulder."

"There are some great exercises and terrific physical therapists who can help you."

"I have plenty of them around the clubhouse."

"Okay...." The beautiful, dark-skinned young woman squatted down to look into the low-slung sports car through the open passenger door. She extended her hand and said, "Hi. My name is Lacey. Our sons hang together. My son is Luke. I've never had a chance to meet you, but I always hear great things about you from Timothy."

He went to extend his hand and abruptly winced in pain. "Sorry. I need to have the trainer look at it today. Thanks for asking. I don't know if I have ever met Luke before. Has he been to my house?"

She smiled. "Your mother is always there when I drop Luke off. You seem to be out of town a lot. Anyways...the boys are great friends."

He started to rub his shoulder again. His indifference to her was noticeable. "Yeah, a lot of traveling is part of my job."

"What do you do, are you in sales?" she inquired.

He looked puzzled. "You don't know who I am?"

Lacey shrugged her shoulders. "No...am I supposed to?"

Terrence started to laugh a little coldly. "I thought maybe your son said something or your husband would have heard of me."

Lacey's smile disappeared. "I don't have a husband. He died nine years ago when Luke was very small." She stood up and said, "It was nice meeting you...whatever your name is...."

Terrence ducked his head down lower so that he could see out of the passenger window. "I'm sorry. My name is Terrence. I'm afraid I'm having a bad day...and now I have to head into L.A."

"Hope your day gets better...." She pushed the door shut with a slightly harder shove than necessary and strolled away.

Terrence rubbed his shoulder with a growing frown and then shoved his car into gear and took off with the sound of screeching tires. As he passed Lacey, she kept on walking with squared-off shoulders and without a glance at him or his fancy car. He looked at his watch and hightailed it down the street so he wouldn't be late to the meeting. Catching the train was something he didn't want to do, but he knew it would get him to his destination faster.

He didn't take the train often. It had been one of his favorite things to do with Timothy and he could see it in his son's face earlier. Timothy and he used to take it to the downtown station and have lunch in Chinatown a few blocks away. Those were the fun days, with no stress or pain, and had been filled with laughter. He had missed out on so much of his son's life the past few years and he had left most of the responsibilities to his mother. She was his rock of Gibraltar and had given him unconditional love and support—never asking for anything in return. He tried his best to give it back, but lately all he could offer was financial security. And that was even on shaky ground. They deserved more. Things definitely had to change.

As he glanced out his window, he made a decision. "I'm going to be a better father and son. I'm going to give them a new me. I'm tired of chasing a career that is literally killing me. I still have a strong body; I'll find a way to make a living without baseball."

He pulled up into the parking lot and sat for a few minutes just thinking of his past. He had made so many mistakes. He had been too selfish to even recognize it for years. Life had seemed to revolve around him, his fans, and the game of baseball.

Jolting himself from his past, he looked at his watch and opened the car door. He tried to get out, but his knee was giving him a hard time. It had locked into place, causing a great deal of pain. Carefully and gradually, he unlocked his knee and slowly slipped out of the car. He walked over to the ticket office and bought a ticket and looked for a vacant seat. The only one left was next to a pretty young woman with a dreamy smile on her face and a couple who were mad for each other. With a sigh, he sat down next to the young woman and began waiting for the train....

# CHAPTER 7

## Enrique

It was still dark outside and Enrique used his floodlight and flashlights to make sure everything was ready to go. His third generation F-series Ford truck with the rustic-style wood siding enclosing the bed was almost as old as Enrique. He was in his late sixties, early seventies—nobody knew for sure, not even him. As old as he was, he still worked morning to night at a business he had built fifty years ago when he was still a young man in his teens. He could still remember the day he had purchased his truck. He could not have been prouder of himself, nor more excited to start his business.

Now so many years later, he prided himself on his old Ford truck that still had the strength and power to get Enrique to work every day. He wouldn't let anyone else drive or repair it. He kept the engine in good condition for all these years by his own capable hands.

Enrique was a humble, honest, and caring man who worked hard and never asked for anything. He was the salt of the earth and everyone knew that he loved his country, God, and his large family. He had come to America as a young man with nothing more than a fistful of dreams and his sixteen-year-old bride. Together, Enrique and Maria raised a family of eight children, six boys and two girls who were given impeccable values. Never one to stray from his Catholic background and deep-seeded principles, Enrique was well respected in his community. It was the love and pride of his family that kept his light shining bright and his heart strong, no matter how many challenges life sent his way.

The flood lights placed strategically around the outside of his modest house gave everyone enough light to get what they needed done in the early morning hours just before dawn. Enrique looked up and saw his two sons. *"Buenos diaz, hijos,"* he said with a grin, taking a sip of his coffee.

Filipe walked toward his dad and stood in front of him. He was a foot taller and carried a very muscular build from all the physical labor he did in the fields. He bent over and put his arm around his father. "It's another great day. You can tell it's not going to be a scorcher." He lifted his hand in the air and the breeze blew through his fingers. "We got everything packed and ready to go, Papa."

Roberto looked at his father and Filipe and smiled. He had carefully watched, over the past few years, how his father was beginning to slow down more and more. Enrique always worked hard and had been doing this all his life and knew exactly what the routine was going to be. It never made

Roberto angry that he couldn't change his father's routine with a new or modern way of doing things, he just let his father continue his old-fashioned methods. Enrique was a man who held a strong constitution of being in charge and making sure everything was done up to his high standards and never settled for less—his livelihood and reputation depended on his quality produce and his word. He was a strong man with his heart open to his community and church when they needed him.

Enrique walked around slowly to make sure everything was tied on securely. Occasionally, he would yank on a rope to insure none of his prized produce could shake loose. That had happened only once in his career—and once was enough. It had been a good lesson to not rely on anyone but himself to secure it. From that day forward, twenty-two years ago, every morning he walked around the trucks making sure his cargo was safe and sound.

He used the flashlight to look at the produce he was taking to the Los Angeles farmers' market to sell to all his loyal customers. They were mostly the large and famous restaurants and some small mom-and-pop grocery stores that would come out early just to seek his seasonal produce and herbs. Some was grown on his farm and a lot more from the farms in his area. His business had started forty-five years ago when he took his pick-up truck and went from farm to farm buying boxes from their premium crops. He would pick up the best of the best from his friends to sell to all his regulars at the farmers' market on a daily basis. Sometimes it was considered a little pricey, but everything was fresh daily and the appreciation of his consumers was what kept his business thriving over all these years.

His successful business had created a decent living that enabled him to support and raise his eight children. Six of those eight were college educated and five had moved away to establish their own lives in fields that ranged from a physician, a chef, a teacher, and a struggling actress. Two of his sons had stayed and were gradually taking over the business.

Maria and Enrique had been married for close to fifty years. They were in their early teens when they met back in Jalisco, just outside of Guadalajara. They lived in the same town and were formally introduced by their parents. It wasn't an arranged marriage, but close.

At first Maria wasn't interested in this energy-filled young man with dreams. But, eventually Maria gave into his youthful enthusiasm as he persistently pursued her. When they were sixteen, they got married with the blessing of their parents in a big church wedding that consisted of the whole town and warm celebration.

Enrique didn't want to stay in the poor town and take over his father's business of shoeing horses and odd jobs. He wanted more and better for Maria and his family. After seeing newspaper articles that offered a better life in the United States, he made a decision to follow those dreams.

With nothing to lose, a chance at making something of his life and providing for his new wife, they both decided to move to California. With the help of family and friends that had connections, they illegally sneaked over the border one dark night. For months they slept in open fields, vulnerable to all kinds of challenges. The only jobs available were working in the fields. Those first few years they worked very hard and saved every penny to create a better life than roaming migrant farmers could ever hope for. Enrique learned as much as he could about farming and at night they both studied English, preparing for the exam to get their citizenship.

When the chance became available and amnesty was offered to the illegal migrants, they jumped at the chance. With all their hard work and studying in night school, they received the most precious papers of their lives—citizenship. With his papers, and very little money in their pockets, Enrique found a small parcel of land he could buy and farm, located outside of Los Angeles in the town of Oxnard. For a few years, he sold his produce off his truck, making stops at all the local markets, restaurants, and street corners until a whole new world opened up and he was asked to participate in the first farmers' market that specialized in organic produce. From that day forward, he delivered his produce to the market and sold it to major distributors, restaurants, and independent gourmet stores. The market opened at five and closed at noon every day. This meant long hours and little sleep as he delivered his trucks filled with perishables. It was an hour drive from his farm, but Enrique didn't mind. He knew he had the best vegetables that vendors were looking for, and his business savvy supplied the rest.

He was humbled as he brought all the farmers in the area together and started this coalition to sell only the best and freshest produce each morning down at the market place. His success was immediate and slowly he made a name for himself within the demanding market. Within a few years it had left him with more than enough eager customers and a thriving business that now supplied produce every morning in his six trucks. Anything that was left over, he drove down to the two missions in Los Angeles to feed the poor. There was no need to bring it home and he knew that there were a lot of starving families who needed it more. He easily remembered those days back in Mexico when money was scarce and his father had a hard time feeding his family or when he first came to the United States how hungry he and Maria sometimes were. The wonderful people in the Ventura Mission had graciously fed them one hot meal a day so they wouldn't starve. He had made a promise to God to give back and help those in need.

Enrique finished securing the truck and went back into the house. He picked up his bagged lunch, kissed Maria goodbye, picked up a box filled with hot cups of coffee and fresh homemade tortillas, and walked out the door with his son, Roberto. At four in the morning, the sky was still dark. Enrique had his schedule timed to coincide with the sunrise and how long it would take to make that fifty mile ride. All five trucks followed in a caravan toward Los Angeles. Roberto, Edwardo, Juan, and Pedro would follow their father to market. Edwardo and Juan always stayed until the market closed. Roberto, Pedro and his father would help drop off the produce and then head home to work the fields.

"*Buenos diaz,*" Enrique said to the men standing around waiting for him to come outside again with their hot coffee. Enrique placed the box on the hood of the truck and hugged each of his workers as they came to grab a cup of coffee and tortillas for the journey into town.

"*Cómo estás?*" Enrique asked each of them, a smile on his face.

This morning the traffic was heavy and Roberto and Enrique were on their way to the mission. They left a little early in hopes of stopping at the hardware shop on the way home. Roberto's truck followed Enrique. He had been watching his father with both eyes, like a circling hawk, over the past few years. Enrique was aging and that had Roberto worried at times. Then, without making it noticeable, he tried his hardest to make his father's workload easier. It was going to be hard when the time came to make his father realize that he needed to slow down. Enrique was a very stubborn man who believed you should die with your work boots on.

The freeway traffic was jammed this morning and the last few miles were moving at a snail's pace. Enrique decided to get off the freeway and take the surface streets for the last ten miles. Roberto followed and together they made a little better time.

As they drove down a quiet neighborhood street, Enrique began to cross over the train tracks, as he had on many occasions. It wasn't a normal crossing where there were major signs, big lights, and the bars that crossed the track as the train went by. It was an old crossing with dirt on both sides of the track and only one cross sign and a single arm that came down to stop traffic. There was graffiti everywhere and the signs were spray painted bright green.

As Enrique slowly crossed the tracks with his front tires, a loud, thunderous noise echoed from under his truck. The truck jolted, jarring Enrique and causing him to hit his head on the front windshield. A little dazed and confused, he sat there for a moment and tried to get his bearings. A loud pounding on the window brought him back to reality. He finally realized where he was and what he was doing. Roberto looked alarmed. Enrique rolled down his window and Roberto watched as a small rivulet of blood ran down the side of his father's face. Without hesitation, Roberto pulled out a rag from his back pocket and wiped the blood off.

"Hey, pops, are you okay? What the hell happened? All of a sudden you stopped dead on the tracks," Roberto said, standing there with questioning eyes.

"I heard a loud popping sound. For a moment I thought it was a loud shotgun. I'm not sure what it was. I know I can't stay on these tracks. The train comes every half hour."

Roberto scrutinized his father's face to make sure he looked okay to drive. "Okay, let's go...."

Enrique nodded and put the truck into drive. He began to gun the engine, but the truck did not move. He couldn't understand why it wasn't moving. The transmission had just been overhauled and was working great. The engine on the truck was continuously maintained so it had plenty of power. *What the hell was holding it?*

"Why isn't this damn truck moving...?" Enrique asked out loud as he opened his door and jumped down to see what the problem was. When he walked around the front of the truck, he noticed that his front tires were completely flat. *"What an odd thing to happen. How did two tires go flat at the same time?"* he said to himself. He stooped lower to take a better look with his old eyes and all he could see was a thick strip of heavy iron. He kicked a flat tire and yelled, "What is this?" He bent further down and tried to move the strip with his weakened hands. For some reason, it had wedged itself between the track and it was lodged deeply into place, making his tires unmovable. Roberto bent down and then stood up and started kicking the heavy iron rod with his heavy boots to try to dislodge it. Nothing was working.

Enrique began to panic and pleaded with Roberto, "We need to get the truck off the track now. A train is due any time. *Hijo*, drive behind me and let's see if we can push it off the tracks." Enrique's voice was beginning to quiver with alarm as Roberto ran back to his truck and slowly tried to line it up with his father's truck. Nothing was working and the bumpers were off. But neither cared. It was not about their trucks or their cargo. It was about a whole six cars of transit riders that were potentially in harm's way. Roberto picked up his cellphone and made an emergency call to try to get some help. With a train due at any moment, he knew he had to do some quick thinking when he was begging for help from the police and fire department. He needed to put them on notice, just in case.

"*Hijo*, I don't care about any damage to the trucks, let's just push it hard to see if we can get it the ten feet we need to clear it off these rails. Don't worry about anything but the people on the train. Hurry...."

Roberto gunned his engine and his back tires began to spin, flinging soft dirt and rocks everywhere. Roberto could not get any traction on his back tires to gain the power to push the larger truck. The truck was like a heavy boulder that would not budge. Roberto and Enrique heard the heavy crushing of metal on metal as Roberto's truck tried to push the other. With the sound of each second ticking off in Enrique's head, his panic turned into terror. Roberto pulled his truck around so that he could push Enrique's truck from the other side to see if he could back the truck off of the tracks, but when Roberto saw the train coming in the distance, he backed up and parked. Feeling sick, he jumped out and ran toward his dad.

By this time there was a growing handful of bystanders, most of them talking on their phones or snapping pictures. Both sides of the tracks were filling with people. Many of the men were desperately trying to help dislodge and push the truck off of the rails.

The whistle of the train, just hundreds of yards away, sounded. The engineer finally realized that the truck wasn't going to move and everyone could hear metal scraping metal as he put his brakes on. The incessant screaming of the brakes sounded like fingernails against a chalkboard.

The high-pitched sound was piercing Enrique's ears, but he was not going to give up. Hell bent on trying, with his last breath he continued to push his gas pedal to the floor and continued to pray. "Dear God, have mercy...."

Roberto grabbed his father's arm and began to pull. "Get out of here," he screamed again and again over all the noise. But his dad did not budge.

"I'm not leaving. I need to get this truck off...." He refused to leave his truck. Like a captain who went down with his ship, his father stood strong, and was willing to become that martyr.

Roberto would not let that happen. Neither would the bystanders. Surrounding men all helped pull Enrique out of the cab of his truck just seconds before it was too late. The train was barreling down the track with its whistle blowing, its brakes screeching, about to collide with a force that could not be measured. That **moment of impact** was like a big tidal wave—and this moment was going to change the lives of everyone it touched. Not one single person was going to walk away unscathed and without a memory that would be embedded in their lives forever....

# CHAPTER 8

## Moment of Impact

Chase and Christie were sitting on the bench hugging and smooching like a pair of lovesick newlyweds. His hands were sliding all over her body, creating laughter and drawing the attention of many of the waiting passengers. Chase didn't care. He was enjoying his morning and looking forward to his afternoon of sexual bliss. He knew nobody would be here to recognize him or Christie. That's why he planned to leave the city and find a more remote place to have their rendezvous. Chase could be calculated and sneaky. With taking the train, Bridget would not be able to check his mileage or his GPS; she had secretly installed an app on her phone for his car.

Yun was sitting across from them, her head resting on the back of the seat and her eyes closed. She could not understand why a couple would unashamedly flaunt 'bedroom antics' in public. She always had a hard time with public displays of affection. She had a bit of an old-fashioned viewpoint. She closed her eyes and began to thinking about all the things she had to get done.

Karyn was sitting with her checkbook in her hands, a dismayed looked on her face as she began to flip through the pages. She was oblivious to everything around her. It had been a tough month and she had no idea how she was going to make her small salary stretch to cover half of her bills, let alone feed her family. Although she had to be appointed a public defender so she could defer the expense of an attorney, it didn't bring her any solace to know that her son was still sitting in Juvenile Hall waiting for the system to hear his case. It didn't make her feel any better knowing that she wasn't a priority to the young attorney who was stacked with cases. She had been at the mercy of the court system her whole life. When she was in foster care as a child, there was no way they could speed up the process—twenty-five years later and still nothing had changed.

Harper was on her own bench with a glowing smile on her face as she flipped through a bridal magazine. Her excitement was so consuming, she was having a hard time containing it. In five days she would become the wife of the only man she had ever loved. He was the most remarkable person, with such a love of life and the world around him. They were a perfect match and she wasn't going to let anything or anyone stop her from wearing her mother's dress and putting on his ring. How many times had she told him that this was going to be the one day in her life she had waited for since she was just a small child? Harper pulled out a piece of paper and began going over her list of things to do. When she was done, she pulled out her cellphone and dialed her sister. The excitement in her voice as she left a message was almost uncontrollable.

Terrence had just stepped onto the platform and was walking toward the ticket counter when the shrill sound of the approaching train caught his attention. Immediately, he looked at his watch and took out his cellphone. He was on the phone when he handed the lady behind the window counter his money. He nodded, picked up his ticket, and walked toward the yellow painted line. The line let the riders know that they could not go past that point as the train approached. All the other commuters were beginning to get off the benches and gather behind the yellow line in hopes of being one of the first to board while others continued to sit patiently. It really didn't matter if you were first or last to board the train. There were plenty of cars and lots of standing room and nobody was ever turned away. This was the line for the first car behind the locomotive. Not many people liked sitting in it because of the engine noise. Others with shorter commutes found it less crowded and more comfortable.

A woman's voice came loudly over the PA system. "Please stand in line and get ready to board; the nine o'clock train is arriving in one minute. Thank you so much for taking Metrolink. Enjoy your ride."

A loud noise pierced the distant air, letting everyone know that the train was pulling into the station. As the shiny silver train stopped, the crowd moved toward the doors with anticipation. Each of the car doors slid open and the riders began to exit. It was a known fact, and a rule of the rails, that exiting passengers had the right-of-way before the new riders could board. Boarding conductors stood on the platform signaling to the all the commuters, making sure everything went smoothly for all the travelers. Security guards walked around keeping an eye on the crowd, looking for anyone who looked suspicious or created any problems.

Because of its tight schedule, the people began quickly entering the cars in single file. Chase and Christie, Yun, Karyn, Harper, and Terrence stood patiently as they stepped into the car closest to their waiting area. It was the first car of the train behind the locomotive. The engineer could be seen through the window as they all boarded and on occasion he would wave. When the engineer held his hand up to the conductor, a final whistle was blown. Last-minute commuters were desperately racing toward the doors in hopes of catching the train, not willing to wait the twenty-five minutes for the next.

As the door was about to close, a young Hispanic boy came running toward the train. Barreling at a speed that only youth could manage, he grabbed ahold of the door with all his strength and pulled himself inside, then he leaned against the closed door trying to catch his breath—gasping for air. He slowly opened his eyes and stared out the window.

Harper glanced out her window and noticed all the police cars with rotating red lights and all the people gathering outside. Her questioning eyes finally dismissed the chaos and she went back to reading her magazine.

José looked scared and disjointed and sweat was dripping off his face. As one tear slipped down his cheek, his hand wiped it clean and a small smile crossed his face.

Maybe he got lucky and his piss-poor attempt at robbing the pharmacy would not catch up with him. He began to question himself. *Did the pharmacy have cameras? Do they have pictures of him? Did his bullet strike anyone? Would they be waiting for him when the train stopped at the station? Would he wind up in jail like his brother...?*

He stood near the door going through the questions that were plaguing his every thought. How was he going to get himself out of this mess he created? What would his mother say? Feeling disorientated and disillusioned, he moved toward the closest seat and sat down.

Harper looked up from her magazine and casually looked around the room. The car was filled to near capacity and everyone seemed settled in. For the next fifteen minutes they would all be sitting in silence listening to the rumbling of the cars as they traveled down the rails to its next destination. The speed was incomprehensible unless you looked out the window. Then you could see how fast the train was going by the blur of the scenery passing by. The train itself had very little movement and the construction and shock absorbers kept the shaking and bouncing to a minimum.

*It's almost like gliding,* Harper thought to herself.

It had not been more than five minutes when all of a sudden, a loud, squealing crash of metal sliding on metal began to fill the room. The engineer blasted the horn non-stop to signify he was having a problem. A back-breaking jolt set the train into a braking motion that set the once passive crowd into a frenzy of fear. The centrifugal force was pulling their bodies toward the back of the car. People began to scream.

Chaos was everywhere, and riders were panicking as the shrill screeching of the brakes continued. Commuters were flying off their seats and landing on each other as debris was flung around with horrendous strength. The power of the force didn't allow anyone to stop what was happening and it didn't allow anyone to gain any control over their own movements. The velocity of the energy created this wind-tunnel that only added to those few seconds of time where pain and panic took over.

Once the brakes had been powerfully applied, the sliding friction force of metal-sliding-on-metal and the gravitational pull had involuntarily thrown everyone on top of each other and to the back of the car. Screams and shrieks, as panic set in, could be heard as the initial contact was made. The tremendous jolt shook the front cars like saltshakers. With a power that could not be explained, the impact of the train hitting something solid created two simultaneous reactions. The two impacts were very close together and only a few seconds apart. The first one was the initial jolt as the train hit something hard and stationary, causing everything and everybody to be thrown back in the opposite direction again. The commuter's bodies were now thrown around the car like a bunch of rag dolls. The second impact was the effect of the cars smashing into each other with an accordion-like response as they were pushed high into the sky and then slammed down onto the ground, causing large chunks of metal and debris to fly everywhere as the derailment continued down through the rest of the cars. The first three cars settled, dust and smoke surrounding them, not far from the track.

When the locomotive crashed, Enrique's truck was pushed a hundred and fifty feet down the track. Immediately, the truck exploded, now a massive fireball, tearing through the engine of the train and into the first car just before it derailed. Two of the cars landed on one side of the tracks and the other cars landed on the opposite end. Screams could be heard everywhere.

One woman's voice screamed, "Help...help...I can't move please help me!"

A man's voice screamed back, "My leg is broken, I need some help...!"

People came running from their houses in the small neighborhood after hearing the loud crashing noise to see if they could help. Devastation was everywhere. Most were afraid to enter the wreckage, but some pushed their way in, searching for anyone they could find.

"Hang in there," a young man screamed. "Keep calling out so we know where you are."

The screams kept coming.

"Over here!"

"No, over here...I can't move!"

"I'm in the second car." was repeated in men's and women's voices from all over the rubble.

Those who could get out on their own were paralyzed with fear as they were slowly escaping from anywhere they could exit from. Others, were in a state of shock and severely injured, and screaming for help. Uncontrollable chaos was everywhere. Panic, fear, and not knowing what to do surrounded the area that was swiftly filling up with passersby and looky-loos. A few bodies, and body parts, were strewn on both sides of the tracks. They had been thrown from the front cars that had been unbelievably crushed. Many survivors, confused and disheveled, were fleeing from the cars like ants crawling out of an ant hill. One-by-one they crawled out of the windows and through the crushed metal—injured and maimed, but lucky to be alive.

"There's more people in that car over there!" one bloodied lady yelled, pointing her hand. The other arm sat dangling uselessly next to her side.

Many of the doors in the cars were jammed and would not open to let the hysterical riders out. "Someone open the doors. We can't get out! Please...please...I beg of you!"

One strong bystander took a large piece of wood and started breaking the car windows out to give a few frantic commuters a way of escaping. Then he coached the battered and disfigured survivors to climb out, "Come on, give me your hands. I'll make sure you get out and get some help. Trust me...." He helped a woman out and handed her off to others. He went back for the next...and the next...making sure they were taken care of. Heroes were showing up everywhere with helping hands and heavy hearts.

A man, with a bone sticking out of his leg, collapsed nearby. Everyone was bloody from shards of glass that were impaled in their skin. Crying and screams continued to fill the air. The smoke from the fireball that destroyed the locomotive was heavy in the air. Sirens grew louder as emergency help finally arrived. The looks on their faces were filled with shock at the carnage they were witnessing.

One EMT yelled to another, "I've never seen anything like this. We need to hurry and get these people to the hospital." He pointed his fingers at the first two cars lying on their sides. "You go to that one and I will take this one." Then he called for assistance. "I need all available help at these two cars. We have lots of injured and some critical!"

The sights and sounds of the crash site was enough to send some over the edge, others just sat there, impassively, not knowing what to do. Others were on their cellphones sending pictures and corresponding with emergency contacts.

Then the sirens began to get closer and closer as the ambulances began to line up. Helicopters began hovering above, shining their floodlights into the darkened carnage. Police sirens, fire trucks, and the hospitals' triage workers were slowly starting to arrive, but with an urgency that had them moving like a stampede of horses. The chaos continued, as screams of victims and the shouts of helpers continued to fill the entire area.

Cries of "Help me...please, help me!" continued to fill the air.

A few of the trained triage specialists, paramedics, nurses, and doctors from the nearby hospitals were beginning to congregate. They immediately set up a triage center that allowed all the medics to sort through the patients and their injuries. This area enabled them to allocate the treatment to those who needed it most, in hopes of maximizing the number of survivors.

A nurse gave out some clean sheets and ordered, "Cover those who died. Don't touch their bodies."

Ambulances were coming and going at a steady pace. Color-coded tarps were spread across the ground. Black, red, yellow, green, and white were filling a large area near the cars and close to the ambulances. These colored tarps each had a meaning and allowed the doctors and nurses a way of sorting the patients according to their urgency.

The black tarp was for the victims that were severely injured and were perhaps not expected to live—most likely to die within the next twenty-four hours. They were the first to leave. The red meant that the patient required immediate surgery or another life-saving intervention. They would have priority for surgical teams and transport to advanced facilities; they could not wait, but were likely to survive with immediate treatment. The yellow indicated observation. Their condition was stable for the moment, but required steady attention by trained persons and frequent re-triage. Green for the 'walking wounded,' those who required a doctor's care, but not immediately—like broken bones without compound fractures or soft tissue injuries. Finally, what everyone hoped for was the white tarp. It was for minor injuries; first aid and home—a doctor's care was not required.

Then came the tags. A few nurse and doctors were yelling, "Make sure you tag them first!"

There were special nurses going to each patient, placing a prefabricated tag on a place that could be seen by the treating doctors. It contained their identity, their assessment, the patient's need for medical treatment, their progress, and any additional information such as pharmaceutical allergies or personal physicians. This was important because the staff of medics was constantly moving from patient to patient and the tag kept them informed.

"This one needs immediate attention and a transfusion!" a doctor yelled at two EMTs. The doctor's hands were covered with blood as he tightened the tourniquet on the patient's wound.

"Send this one to the red tarp," a nurse yelled.

A doctor told his attendant, "This one is yellow. Watch him closely."

Even with all the commotion, everything was still done in an orderly and disciplined manner. Dr. Ron Lambert was the head doctor in control and barking out the orders. Nobody had an ego or took offense to anyone who was pushing their authority to get things done. Lives were at stake and there were so many severely injured. They had already counted six deaths and they were sure there were more. A few of the injured were teetering on the edge. All of the deaths came from the front three cars. The car that was attached to the locomotive was where most of the motion and impact was absorbed. The locomotive was fractured into a thousand little pieces and what was left was molten steel from the explosion and fire. They were sure the engineer was dead but could not account for the body yet. The sight in front of everyone was gruesome.

Immediately, the scene began to open up to hundreds of people who had invaded the small neighborhood just to get a glimpse of the carnage. Police were putting up barriers to stop and control the influx of the growing crowd and vans filled with news reporters.

Police were shouting, "Get back. Give the emergency workers some room. This is not a circus people...this is life or death! Stay behind the caution tapes.... Don't make us arrest you!"

Every reporter wanted a story and most would do anything for the horrific pictures of the graphic scene in front of them. The media circus was starting and the sensationalism of the disaster was beginning to spin into a different kind of chaos. Reporters were getting pushy in their need to be the first to have their station supply information to the public. Helicopters and drones were circling above the doctors and nurses who were trying their best to concentrate on the victims. Privacy was non-existent as all of the television stations began to air their breaking coverage.

Nothing was sacred, and every passenger was fair game to the correspondents. One passenger who was sitting on the ground with blood dripping down his face described the gruesome scene just moments after impact. "People were scattered all around the car...blood everywhere...we kept screaming for help."

Another reporter had a woman explaining, "It happened so fast...we didn't have time to brace for the crash." Then she inhaled deeply and said, "we landed on the floor and I suddenly saw flames shooting up yards from my head...."

The police finally pushed the reporters to a contained and controlled area, away from those who were wounded.

Two large black trucks pulled up with NTSB and FRA in florescent white letters on them. The police opened up the barrier and let them into the crash area. The NTSB was the National Transportation Safety Board and the FRA the Federal Railroad Association. They were there to conduct independent investigations of the crash site to determine the probable cause of the accident. Reports on the details about the accident, analysis of the factual data, conclusions, and the probable cause of the accident were required. The investigators began to file out of the truck and look around. Wearing orange vests to signify who they were, they began to sift through the area with an intensity that would get them the answers they were looking for. Everything in the surrounding area was being investigated. Law enforcement were there to look for any criminal causes and were conducting an investigation of their own. The fire department had their investigators there to look for clues involving the explosion and fire. Eventually all the reports would secure everything they needed to know.

Right now all they knew was that an old vegetable truck was stuck on the track. Unfortunately, the name of the owner of the truck and everything about him and his family was already being spread through the media and streaming across the television and radio stations.

# CHAPTER 9

**THE AFTERMATH:**
*Who lives and who dies...and where do their lives go from here....*

## Chase

It had been a very long day and it was only noon. Bridget had appeared at the courthouse for a pre-trial assessment and then rushed back to the office for two meetings with potential clients and one deposition. She had a client coming in who was pretty rattled about her pending divorce. She was hoping to defer her anger and pass her through the office with the smallest amount of aggravation and dramatics. When the actress was mad, there was no telling what her reactions would be or what melodrama would be staged. Bridget knew this case was going to be long and drawn out and it probably would not end well. This was the high-powered and intense clientele she dealt with, and her cool and decisive demeanor was what kept them coming back and referring her to the endless supply of the industry's marriage debacles.

This actress was married to a well-known actor who looked like a saint in public, but had a dark side. Bridget had sent out the letter of complaint, and the repercussions were starting to create a barrage of bullets she had to dodge constantly. Bridget had her paralegal immediately draw up a restraining order and was requesting a protection order. She was fixing to hit him with a temporary order for child support and alimony. If that didn't set him walking on the straight and narrow, she was going to have to pull out something else from her bag of tricks.

Bridget was sitting at her desk and she opened her drawer to pull out a large bottle of ibuprofen and antacids. Her headache had started early in the morning when she had the confrontation with Chase and turned into a migraine when the court postponed the hearing. The continual grinding of her job and her marriage falling apart were beginning to take their toll on her health. She could feel it and the kids could see it. Chase couldn't care less. His narcissistic and self-absorbed behavior was getting out-of-control and Bridget was too busy to deal with it.

Chase had not started their marriage as a self-centered son of a bitch. At least, she couldn't see it then. Nowadays, he didn't pay much attention to the boys or to her. Their fights were always about him needing to accept his fatherly responsibilities and his reluctance to help out with simple tasks around the house. Lately he was starting fights in front of the kids and neighbors and friends. He just didn't care. It seemed like he had checked out of their marriage and was selfishly taking care of his own needs and wants.

Even at work the anger and hostility still occupied her mind. Bridget opened the lid of the ibuprofen as her head began to pound harder than ever.

*Gawd, I don't know how much more I can take from Chase?* she said to herself. *I have everything resting on my shoulders and all he can think about is himself.*

Bridget washed down the pills with a cold cup of coffee that had been sitting at her desk since she got to the office. She barely had time to even take a sip or two. And now, the rest of the day was filled with more aggravation from numerous clients. She was walking on a thin edge and she didn't know how much more it would take to make her jump off.

David walked into the office with a smile on his face as he handed her a stack of papers. "What else do you need me to do right now?"

"Book me a vacation...." She sat back in her chair, laid her head back, and closed her eyes.

"I bet you would like Bora Bora. You know...where the soft ocean breezes caress your face and there is no civilization to bother you. If you're lucky, you can sleep the days away listening to the waves splashing up onto the white sand. "

David began to hum *Aloha 'Oe*. He brought his arms up and began to dance the hula as he continued to hum the song.

Bridget opened one eye and began to smile at his silly antics. For the first time in a long while, she could find the humor in a conversation. "That would work...."

"Want me to book it?" He lifted his eyebrows while waiting for her answer.

"Thanks, David, you made my day." She smiled. "You do so much for me already. I don't know what I would do without all your help and your crazy sense of humor. I'm not an easy person to work for."

"Who feeds you that crap? I enjoy having you as a boss...."

"So, what's up for the rest of the day?" Bridget sighed softly, feeling a little bit better.

"Did you hear about the big train crash in Los Angeles this morning? Holy smokes, so far they have six or eight deaths and haven't even begun to sift through the horrible wreckage."

Bridget pinched her eyebrows together. "No, I haven't heard anything at all. I'm so out of the loop on days like today! I've been concentrating on Marilee and her pending divorce. I've never seen so much drama—and I know there's so much more to come."

"How did you miss it? It's all over the news and radio; the media blitz is going crazy. I bet the whole city of Los Angeles is glued to the coverage."

Bridget shrugged her shoulders and shook her head. "Clue me in, David. You're my eyes and ears. What happened? And spare me all the drama. I've had enough for one day!"

"Some idiot's truck got stuck on the tracks. They don't know if it was an accident or intentional. You never know nowadays with all the crazies out there. They're either looking for their fifteen minutes of fame or they are just going to take innocent people down with them. You see this throughout our country with the random shooting. Hell, sometimes I'm afraid to go to the movies!"

He walked over to the unique wall-to-wall cabinet and opened up a set of doors. Inside was a flat-screen television that was used for watching videos from their clients.

He turned it on and immediately Bridget's eyes widened at the ghastly pictures coming from the live coverage of the site. Destruction was everywhere.

"I've been to that crossing many times. It's a fast way to get to work and it's nestled in a small neighborhood. Sometimes I see kids playing on those tracks! Wow...."

"Me too...."

She stood up and came around the desk, her eyes opened as wide as saucers. Her jaw dropped open as they both stood directly in front of the television and stared at the anchor. He was giving the viewers information they were transmitting on a moment-to-moment thread.

"Oh my god...." she mumbled.

"That is crazy...." David said.

Everything was being broadcast from all directions and it looked like it was coming from a movie. Sirens, ambulances, fire truck, helicopters, and medical people filled the screen.

Then they heard the anchorwoman say, "They have confirmed six deaths and so far sixty-four are injured—seventeen in critical condition. We will update numbers as soon as we get more information. Please stay tuned with our minute-to-minute coverage."

Bridget's phone rang and it abruptly broke their attention to the chaos they were witnessing on television. With a brisk walk, she picked up the phone. "Hello."

The first thing she heard was a deep baritone voice. "This is Captain Brooks. I need to speak with Chase Walker's next of kin."

Bridget froze, her eyes wide, as she intently listened to the police officer on the other end of the phone.

It took her a minute to find her voice.

"Ma'am? Are you there?"

Bridget gripped the edge of her desk tightly and asked as carefully as she could manage, "What do you mean his wallet was found at the crash site? You must have made a mistake. Are you sure you're calling for the right Chase Walker? I know there are a few men in the area that have the same name as him."

She held the phone tight to her ear and listened to the answer. Her face was red and her heart was beating a mile a minute.

"You're sure?" she questioned again.

She listened silently as she started to pace around the office. David only heard parts of the conversation. He watched her, confused and concerned.

"But he is at work...." she mumbled, as a gnawing fear set in.

Bridget swung around and turned toward David. She held the phone between them and placed it on speaker. They listened to the police officer on the other end of the phone confirm their doubt with a driver's license he was holding in his hand. David stood there with an astonished look on his face, shaking his head in disbelief.

"His boss said he had the day off? Really? Okay, let me take down some of this information." Frantically, Bridget picked up a pad of paper and began writing furiously with her shaking hand. "St. John's hospital?" Bridget hung up the phone and began to panic. She ran to her small closet and pulled out her purse and turned to look at David.

Anger and suspicion were written all over her face. "David, will you let my father know, and tell him to have my mother pick up the boys from school immediately before they hear or see anything that will scare them."

David moved within inches from Bridget and said, "I'll pick them up if you want."

"No...get my mother, and they can spend the night there. I will call from the hospital and tell her everything. Also, cancel all my appointments. Tell them an emergency came up that was unavoidable."

David wrote it down on a note pad. "Anything else?" David looked up with sad eyes. "I hope he's not one of the casualties."

Bridget ground her teeth together. "I've got to go."

Bridget picked up her cellphone and tried to call Chase. His phone went directly to voicemail. Bridget left a breathless message, "Please give me a call as soon as you get this." Most of the time he didn't call her back for hours.

She looked up at David with questioning eyes. "Why would that fucker be on that train? Where the hell was he going? Have I been that stupid, David?"

David didn't say anything. He just pointed to the door before he took the liberty to answer that obvious question. "Go...."

Bridget went out the door looking confused and scared.

There was nothing but chaos at the hospital. People were everywhere. The outside was lined with television trucks and reporters. They were voraciously giving the news channel all the drama the accident could hoard. Sympathetic interviews with family members they cornered in this chaos were being spun in all directions as many of their loved ones laid injured and dying in the upper rooms. Firemen, police, nurses, and doctors were seen going from room to room in the emergency triage center they set up inside the hospital within the first few minutes of the crash. The waiting areas were standing room only. The deep seriousness of the event showing on all the sorrowful faces of those hoping to get news on their loved ones.

Bridget walked up to a small information desk. The young woman was giving out information to each of those looking for their loved ones. Her desk was cluttered with stacks of papers that had been updated and accumulated over the past few hours. All this was beyond her comprehension and her focus was to prove them wrong with their speculation.

*"He couldn't have been on that train,"* Bridget kept repeating to herself.

Bridget waited patiently. When it was her turn, she looked directly at the young lady. "I got this call, but I do think there has been a mistake. They said my husband was on the train, but I'm sure he was at work. Maybe you can look up his name and clear up this mistake once and for all." She smiled. "His name is Chase Walker."

The young lady's finger slowly went down each list until she suddenly came to a stop. She took a scrap of paper and wrote down some information and handed it to Bridget. "He's on the third floor." She opened a small drawer and took out a pass that dangled from a safety pin. "Just pin this onto your sweater, then take the elevator upstairs and someone can help you from there. Look for the lady with the clipboard." Her sad face reflected the day.

Bridget began to stutter. "There has to be a mistake. It can't be him."

The young woman shook her head. "Third floor. They will be able to help further."

*How many times has that young lady heard the same response from family members?* Bridget wondered.

Bridget inhaled a deep breath and let it go slowly as she took the papers and tag from the young lady's hand. While the realization that this was actually happening began to set in, she walked over to the bank of elevators. Small groups of people were waiting for one of the doors to open. Her eyes began to focus on a young man and his family. She could see by their faces that their grieving process had already begun. An older woman was hysterically crying as the young man pulled her tight against his chest to comfort her. His eyes were filled with tears, but his strength showed as the elevator doors opened. He gathered his group and slowly began herding them inside. Bridget was too shaken to move. Fear had taken over and she instinctively moved over to another door, unable to get into the same elevator as the bereaved family.

When she finally made it upstairs, panic began to set in. She walked into a waiting room filled with several small groups of people. Blindly making her way across the room, she heard a loud, angry voice in the corner amongst a gathering of family. The younger man in the other elevator was standing and yelling at an older man. "I have no idea why she was with him! But I will get to the bottom of this once and for all. She was supposed to be at work!"

Suddenly, a police officer entered the room and began to assist the angry man out. His family followed as they were taken to a closed door and were led into that room.

Terrified and bewildered at the whole scene in front of her, Bridget walked over to a nurse holding the clipboard in her hand.

"I'm looking for Chase Walker," Bridget said, as she handed the nurse the note from downstairs.

The nurse looked at Bridget and asked, "Are you family or friend?"

"Wife," she spit out venomously.

The nurse backed up a little when she heard the anger coming from Bridget. "Thank you. "We are only allowing immediate family in right now, until things settle down. He's in room 310-A. I'll send a doctor in to explain what his injuries are before you enter, so you know what to expect. "

"Thank you," Bridget whispered.

Bridget moved down the hall and slowly opened the door. Chase was heavily sedated. She saw all the tubes and medical equipment attached to his body. One leg was up in the air, in a sling-like contraption hanging from the ceiling. His arm, from his wrist to his shoulder, was in a L-shaped cast. Contusions and bruising covered his face, almost making him unrecognizable. Bridget stepped through the door to take a better look.

Shortly, the doctor walked in. He extended his hand, and sighed. His deep voice was low as he spoke. "I'm so sorry. The lady your husband was with just passed away. Her family is quite distraught and my condolences—"

Abruptly, the door opened and the man that had been yelling in the waiting room came flying through it. He was screaming, "That fucking son of a bitch! Look what he did to my wife! I'm going to kill him, like he killed her—"

Three orderlies came rushing through the doors to stop him from attacking Chase while he laid helplessly in bed unconscious. The man's screaming didn't faze Chase, who had been heavily sedated, but it had frozen Bridget to the floor and left her shaking like a scared mouse. When they finally got the frenzied man out, the doctor put his arm around Bridget's shaking body and led her outside. In the distance, she could still hear that man yelling and screaming obscenities about Chase.

The doctor squared her shoulders and looked directly into her eyes. "I'm so sorry. I...this is not a good way to find out that your husband was with another woman. I just presumed it was work related or a family friend."

Bridget stood there stoically. She was just trying to absorb the last tumultuous half hour. She looked at the doctor. "I'm sorry you were put in the middle. I'm sorry I'm in the middle. As you can see, I'm at a loss for words...." She took a deep breath. "Is he expected to live?"

"Well, I want you to know that Chase is very fortunate and he will recover. He's got a lot of broken bones, but he did survive the fatal crash that took the lives of many in that first car. He will not be able to play golf again and he will have a slight limp, along with a few more limitations. He was saved by an emergency surgery removing his spleen before he bled to death. He's lucky to be alive. Again, I'm sorry. If there is anything I can do, just let me or the staff know."

Bridget said, "I'm not so sure how lucky this day has been for him. Thank you, doctor. I'm going home to absorb all this crap that has been placed on my shoulders!" Bridget turned and walked back toward the elevators.

She left the hospital that first day, dazed, and had lots to think about. While the children were up in their rooms at her mother and father's mansion, Bridget was trying to sort out her life.

She sat in her car away from everything and everybody. For an hour, she watched the crowds of people and observed all the chaos that surrounded the crash. Quietly, she was trying to figure out some unanswered questions—there were no answers to be found. As a wife and an attorney, she knew exactly where she was going to find them. She went to his office. A few discreet employees stepped forward and expressed their apologies, along with confessions of his affair with his secretary. They were terribly distraught over Christie's death. Bridget found all she needed to know. The trip to Vegas, many afternoons off, a trip to Mexico that was planned, and this afternoon's rendezvous had left Christie dead and virtually gave Bridget no other choice.

With all the information she had accumulated, her heart sank deeper and deeper into despair. She had tried so hard to keep her marriage going for the boys, but learning that Chase had been having an affair with his young secretary who had only been married for a year was despicable. Bridget had a lot of decisions to make—this crash had finally opened her eyes.

For over a week, Bridget did not go to work or answer any calls. When she finally decided what she needed to do, it was almost like a weight being lifted off her shoulders. A weight she had been dragging around for the past five years. Her mother and father listened, but never said a word. These were decisions that could only be made by her.

Bridget walked back into the hospital. Things had settled down. The waiting rooms were still full from the family and friends of the injured, but the news hounds were limited to the outside of the hospital. They recognized Bridget from the many newspaper clippings and articles she had been in over the years pertaining to her famous clients, but she refused to stop and feed them any information.

During the week, many stories had leaked out. Rumored speculation was encircling the frenzied sharks as they waited to come up with their next big story. They had reported on Chase and his affair, the death of his newlywed girlfriend, and were fed intimate details by Chase's coworkers who were not shy about answering questions. Bridget and Chase ended up on the front cover of many trash magazines—but Bridget couldn't care less. Her only concern now was that the children did not get pulled into the circus.

She was forced to keep the kids away from the television and had to take them out of school. Her fear that one of their friends at school would taunt or tease the boys, leaking the sordid reality of Chase's adultery was constantly a threat. She brought in a teacher to homeschool them. And it was working so far. All except Josh. He knew exactly what was going on and he watched silently from a distance.

The repercussions of the crash had left Bridget's head spinning in circles as she tried to figure out how to keep her family together. What hurt Bridget the most was that Chase never gave it a second's thought as he romanced his secretary. He never considered her or the kids. The past week had left her with plenty of time to think about what her next move would be. *Would she stay or would she take the boys and leave?*

Bridget had not been back to see Chase since the first day she was there. If he was a big enough boy to get himself into this mess, then he could damn well get himself out. Nothing he could have said or done at any point in time could ever minimize what he had done. Chase had tried calling, and when that didn't work, he had texted her a few times. Her texts were always short and clipped. *'The boys are fine.' 'I'm okay.' 'Feel better.' 'See you soon.'*

Bridget stepped out of the elevator and strolled over to the nurse's station. A young blonde nurse was sitting behind the desk, typing on the computer. She looked up and smiled.

Bridget stood silently in front of the counter. "Excuse me, could you tell me what room Chase Walker is in? I heard they moved him."

The nurse smiled. "Yes, ma'am. He's in 305. He requested a private room. Are you family? I haven't seen you here before. Sorry, I have to ask everyone, because we had a lot of deceptive reporters sneaking in."

Bridget whispered, "I'm his wife." She leaned on the counter and elevated her voice a little. "How is his recovery going?"

"He's one of the more demanding patients. That's why we moved him into his own room." She smiled and rolled her eyes. "Actually, he's doing quite well, considering the circumstances. I think the doctors said he might be able to go home soon. You might need someone to help you get him in and out of bed the first few weeks, because of his broken leg and hip. But you can talk to his doctors and they will give you all that information."

Bridget sweetly smiled and began to walk down the hall looking for room 305. There was no need to take her anger out on a hardworking nurse. She was calm and collected, and completely relieved she had taken the past week off from work. She needed a few days to sort things out and decide how she was going to handle this. She had watched this kind of despicable behavior by her clients and their spouses, but had never thought she would be sitting in the middle of such betrayal. Chase had stepped completely over the line.

Over that week, Bridget had explained to her sons that their daddy had been in that big train accident and while he was healing in the hospital, they were going to stay with their grandmother and grandfather. The little ones didn't care or understand, but the older son, Josh, seemed to know that something was terribly wrong. Bridget knew she was going to have to sit down with him and explain what she was doing. That would come after she talked to Chase.

As she walked down the hall, she could still remember the first day very vividly as she left the hospital more than angry. She felt her world was spinning off its axis. That very moment, when she had seen Chase laying there helpless, and then Christie's angry husband crashed into the room making horrible accusations—her life stood still. He was not at work. He was on his way to Laguna Beach by train with his secretary for a day at a fancy Hotel to romp at the beach and in bed.

Bridget briskly knocked on the door, as if he was a stranger. He yelled, "Just fucking come in!"

Bridget opened the door and stepped in. "Hello, Chase, I can see nothing has changed. You're still as pugnacious as ever."

Chase's face turned red and he sat back and relaxed. "I thought you were the physical therapist." He inhaled a deep breath and slowly exhaled. "I've been waiting a week to talk to you. Why haven't you come to see me or brought the boys? I'm pretty pissed."

Bridget didn't trust herself, so she moved the chair close to the door and sat down and crossed her legs. She willed herself to stay calm. "No need to come see you. I learned so much at your office that there was nothing really left to say to each other. Vegas, days off, Mexico; how long was this going on? Did you ever think about the children and how this would affect them? Forget me...what about them?" Her voice raised up with hurt.

His voice softened. "I'm sorry, Bridget. We were just having a tough time in our marriage and I was so beside myself. Somehow I just fell into this. She meant nothing. I love you.... I want to start over. I really want to make this up to you and the boys."

It has been years since she heard any softness in his voice or those three words. The years had passed and their lives had changed.

With a smooth and composed voice, he said, "I love you, babe. And I'm sorry." He held out his arms. "Come over here and sit next to me. Let's start over and work this out. We'll go to therapy like everyone does nowadays and find a way...."

Bridget knew his words were meaningless. He had been caught and he was fighting not to lose what he had. She tilted her head and eyed him coldly. "I want a divorce."

His face turned red and he gulped for air. "Come on, Bridge. We can get through this. What about the boys?"

Bridget laughed. "What about the boys...?"

He was looking nervous. "We need to keep it together for them. How many times do you want me to say 'I'm sorry'?"

"Sorry...? You haven't thought about 'them' for a long time," her venomous words were spit out slowly and evenly, "or you would not have publicly embarrassed and humiliated us. You just got caught and now you are sitting with your hand in the cookie jar trying to weasel your way out of any kind of discipline."

He shook his head. "I want to see my sons!"

Bridget stood up. "No!"

He yelled, "What do you mean, no?"

Bridget walked closer to the bed. "My father put the house up for sale. After all, it is his. It was his down payment and it was put in his name. We were just renters!"

"What...?" he screamed. "I paid the rent on that house for over twelve years!"

Bridget shook her head. "No—I paid the rent, out of my own checkbook, for twelve years."

His anger was rocketing and he grimaced when he tried to sit up. "It's half my home...."

"We never changed the title and the courts only recognize what is in writing."

His jaw dropped in disbelief.

"I've had a moving company pack all your things in boxes and everything is in the garage. Maybe your mother can help you find a place to live while you are here. If there is anything you want—make a list. When you get released in a few weeks, I will have it all moved to your new place. For anything else, you can talk to my attorney."

"Look, babe.... Don't do this. We can make it work."

"I've worked my ass off for you long enough." She laid the divorce papers on the bed. "Consider yourself served."

"You can't do this."

Bridget turned her back on him and walked toward the door, and then turned around for one last time. "You're wrong. Consider it done." She smiled. "Don't know what you're going to do with the golf cart. The doctor said you won't be able to play anymore because of your broken hip. And you should check your mail. I think you've been fired. Somewhere in your company's policies there is a paragraph that states employees cannot fuck each other." Bridget opened the door and walked out.

As Bridget was walking down the hall she thought about her talk with her father the night before.

*"You're a big girl now. You have worked your fingers to the bone to provide for your family and I suspect you will continue. This time my only hope is that you look at your boys and put them first. This lesson was a hard one on how to balance. Work out what kind of hours you want at the office and if you don't want to come back...that's okay too! It's time to think about yourself."*

She didn't want a damn thing from Chase. All she wanted was to cut her hours at the firm, downsize her home, and learn how to take those few hours off when needed. Most of all, she never wanted to miss any more of her sons' soccer games.

# CHAPTER 10

## Harper

Austin was at work when a text message came in that said, *'Call your mother, ASAP!'*

He smiled to himself as he continued to deal with some disgruntled students. One young woman tried to get him to change her grade with promises of better attendance the next semester. Rarely did he change a grade once it had been posted. He was a very systematic professor, and he always kept a competent set of marks—most with expedient comments. On occasion, if he realized that a student had really tried harder or came in many times for help, he would give them the benefit of the doubt. The student that had just left was one of those lucky ones. She had pleaded her case and convinced Austin to slip the grade up by a half of a point.

It was nearing noon and Austin was starving. When he stopped at Starbucks on his way to school this morning, he only ordered coffee. While he paid for his coffee, he could hear Harper's lecture on the necessity to eat a healthy breakfast. But sometimes he just wasn't hungry. With hunger gnawing at his belly now, he was going to the cafeteria.

A text came in again and his cellphone began to chime. *'Call me, please.'*

Austin loved his mother, but she had become very overbearing with the upcoming wedding. Although his parents had offered to pay for half of it, the Puzzio's had graciously declined. Leona, his mother, thought she would be a bigger part of the plans if the contribution was larger. Unfortunately, it had not worked out the way she wanted. Instead, Camilla had given her a few things to do and the rest was already taken care of by their large family. Camilla and Leona got along great except when Leona overstepped her bounds and tried to take over. She could be a little bossy and at times very insistent on doing things her way. With eight children, she had to take those reins in her hands and hold on tight—it wasn't easy.

During Austin's approaching nuptials he had been forced to rein her in a little in the best way he knew how. He loved his mother too much to intentionally hurt her feelings. With Austin being the first of her children to get married, she had many lessons to learn and taking a backseat was the hardest one.

Austin sat down with his sandwich and chips, then pulled out his phone to call his mother. "Hey, Mom, what's up?"

Without saying hello and sounding very distraught, she choked out, "Have you heard from Harper? I'm very worried."

Austin responded to his mother's hysterics. "Mom, calm down, you sound a mess. She's okay. She took the train into L.A.

today to pick up her dress. She had lots to do. I left her at the apartment and she told me she had taken off the morning from work and is taking a later shift." He groaned into the phone. "Boy, I can't wait until this wedding is over. Everyone is so edgy this week. I just want everything to go back to normal. God only knows what it will be like with a baby on the way!"

Leona gasped. "But what train did she go on?"

Austin grumbled again. "Mom, what is your problem today? Calm down, everything is fine."

She yelled into the phone, "There's been a train crash in Los Angeles. I can't get any information, please make sure Harper was not on that train." Her last few words came out so rushed that they were barely recognizable.

He whispered, "What? I'll call you back...." He immediately hung up.

He lifted his briefcase to the table, taking out his iPad, and then went to the search engine. What he saw knocked the breath out of his lungs. *Six dead and sixty-four injured.* Austin grabbed his iPad in one hand, briefcase in the other, and ran towards the door. He didn't know what to do or who to contact, but he had the sinking feeling that his fiancé was on that train and he needed to know where she was. He looked at his phone and there were no messages from Harper, which was unusual. She didn't usually call or text. He dialed her immediately and it went directly to service. He texted her and still nothing. Then he began to panic.

He called her sister.

"Hello, this is Hilary."

Paranoia was reflected through his voice. "Hil, this is Austin. Harper was coming into

L.A. today, right? Have you heard from her yet? Is she with you?"

Hilary sounded confused. "No.... She said she would call once she got her dress. Why, what's up? I just figured it would be a late lunch because the seamstress was still working with her on the dress."

His breathing intensified. "There's been a big train crash in L.A." He paused for a second as his mind began to spin. "Shit, I was hoping she was with you. I should have heard from her by now."

Alarm began to creep into in Hilary's voice. "I'm going to call around. I am friends with a lot of law enforcement. I'll call you back. Give me a few minutes!"

"I'm going to call around too!"

The phone disconnected.

Austin spent the next half hour on the phone, but learned very little. He kept getting the same run around from everyone he contacted. Not a lot of information about the injured yet. Nothing was given out unless you were immediate family. However, they did give out the name of the hospitals the injured were being transported to.

He sat there and gave it some thought. *I don't want to call her parents and alarm them unnecessarily. Not until I hear from Harper. No need to throw everyone into a panic. Maybe she didn't take the train. Maybe she decided to take her car, because she was running off schedule or maybe she made extra stops.* He kept giving himself reasonable excuses.

He called Hilary back. "Heard anything?"

"No. Neither have my parents or her work." She sighed. "I thought maybe they called her in unexpectedly."

"Hilary, meet me at one of the hospitals? I think we will find out more information there than sitting on the phone."

"Sure, I'm out the door right now."

Austin had to park blocks away because of the media circus. He was barely able to get in the front doors because of the interrogations. When they finally let him in, he let out a deep sigh.

The lobby was packed with hundreds of people all waiting for any information about their loved ones. There was a small table set up as the information desk located in the center of the lobby. A line of worried people were standing patiently for their turn to ask questions and find answers. Austin got into the long line and stood there nervously shuffling his feet. As the chatter around him intensified, he faced the front door, looking for Hilary or Harper to walk in. When he finally saw Hilary and Camilla, Hilary and Harper's mom, he yelled Hilary's name and waved his arms high in the air. Once their eyes met, they ran over and hugged him.

In a shaky voice, she asked, "Have you heard anything? Do they have a list of the injured? They said on the news that there were nearly seventy people injured, some critically."

He lifted up his hand and looked at his cellphone again. "Not a word, text, or anything."

"I'm not worried about that. She could have lost her purse or left her cellphone at home. You know Harper...she sometimes doesn't think...." Camilla smiled shakily.

"I wish they would have sent some of the injured to her hospital. At least they know her there and that would give us an edge," he said.

"Me too, but this is a huge teaching facility and it has all the best doctors for trauma. The victims couldn't be in a better place. Plus they have other facilities off campus they can disperse them to. I have her best friends at work helping us get some information."

They continued to wait in line. Austin turned around to look at the big clock in the lobby when he noticed his mother jogging toward him. With mixed emotions, he held out his arms and gave her a hug. "I didn't want a lot of people here until we found out something. What if she's okay and is running extra errands around town and we are stressing over nothing?"

Leona let go of Austin and said, "I couldn't sit at home and just wait. Your father thought I should come down and see for myself that she was okay. I hope we are overreacting."

Nobody said a word as they stood in line for an hour. Their faces showed the uneasiness from just being in the surroundings and knowing the possibilities. The mothers kept busy talking about the wedding.

Cheryl tapped Austin on the shoulder and slipped into his outstretched arms when he turned around and recognized her. She was Harper's best friend and they worked at the same hospital on the same floor. They had been friends since middle school, were roommates in college, and now she was going to be the maid of honor for her dear friend.

Cheryl's face looked red and heartrending. Everyone turned to look at her, and she asked, "Have you heard anything?"

Everyone shook their heads negatively.

Austin backed up to look into Cheryl's eyes. He noticed a sadness he'd never seen before. He asked, "You found something out, didn't you?"

Cheryl took out her hospital identification tag from her pocket and pinned it to her nurse's uniform. "Stay here for a moment." She left the group and walked over to a closed door and walked through it.

Austin sighed. "If anyone could find out anything, it would be Cheryl. She's a very tenacious nurse, just like my Harper!"

The televisions were on in the lobby, but the sound had been turned off. They were all watching the anchor as he walked through the crash site still filled with all the emergency personnel. Helicopter views filled the screen as they all stood there listening to the ambulances pulling into the back doors of the hospital. The view from the sky was daunting as the helicopters kept circling around the crash site. The first five cars of the train had derailed and turned on their sides. Wreckage was everywhere. Two of them had been nearly demolished and the locomotive was almost unrecognizable.

Austin moaned, "Oh my god, how did this happen? Why did this happen?"

The screen switched to a completely disintegrated truck that had been pushed down the track a hundred and fifty feet by what was left of the locomotive. You could barely see anything that indicated what it was, except for the front tires. Emergency workers surrounded it and the NTSB was already on the scene sifting through the wreckage and combing the area for any information on the crash. They were wearing shirts that were very noticeable, even on television. Onlookers filled the area in every direction they could, held back by law enforcement. Some were helping with the injured, others just watching the morbid scene as it began to unfold.

Camilla, who was a practicing Catholic and went to Church every Sunday, had her hands clasped together and was praying as she watched the grim scenes on the television. The eeriness of her praying and the prattling sounds from the crowd was making Austin feel a little uncomfortable. Abruptly, loud wails and screams came from the other end of the waiting room. The rest of the room became silent as everyone watched. One family had been given the worst news of all. Immediately, the family was ushered through a door and into another room for privacy.

Cheryl came out the door and walked toward their small family. When she stood in front of them, she quietly said, "Follow me."

She took Austin's hand and the rest followed as she went back through the same door she had just came out of. Without a word, she left them standing in an empty, white sterile room as she walked through yet another door marked 'personnel only.' The look on Austin's face did not go unnoticed as the group stood in the room waiting to find out if Harper was on that train. The sooner they found out, the sooner they could be with her. That was all Austin wanted, the only thing he could focus on at the moment. He wanted to be by her side, holding her hand and kissing her lips, telling her like he had a thousand times before how much he loved her.

Austin looked at his mother whose eyes spoke of a mother's worry. He said, "I just want her to be alive. Anything else I can deal with."

She looked up at her son and smiled. "She's fine. They just have so much going on with all the chaos and casualties that getting all their information together is hard. It's only been a few hours."

He shook his head, a little perturbed. "It's been over six hours, Mom. They have everything under control. They practice these emergency triages all the time to be prepared in case...."

She put her hand on his shoulder and began to rub soothingly in a circular motion. That always calmed him down as a small boy. "Identifying all those on the train and working with the injured and notifying the families takes painstaking time for everyone involved."

He wiped away the tears before they slid down his face. "Six have been confirmed dead.... Please, let her be okay. I don't know what I would do...if anything happened to her."

Hilary was standing nearby and heard the conversation. She stepped closer. "We don't even know if she was on the train. She may still be in her fitting or trying to find a way home because all of the other trains are closed down."

Austin pulled his cellphone out of his pocket and held it up. "What about returning our calls?"

"Well...you know my sister as well as me. She leaves her phone on the kitchen counter and walks out the door all the time."

He opened his phone and skimmed through his calls and texts. A slight smile crossed his face for the first time in the past few hours since this horrible nightmare had started. "Well, you could be right. I haven't got anything in my phone from her since I walked out our front door." His shoulders began to relax a little.

Both the mothers were standing next to each other, holding hands. Camilla had her eyes closed and kept silently praying. Leona was inhaling deeply and slowly exhaling in an even rhythm. The room was deathly quiet and empty. There was a table with eight chairs in the middle and another eight chairs that lined the walls. But, everyone was standing in a small circle in one corner of the room.

"This must be a conference room of some type," Austin said as he looked around, not knowing what else he could do to hold on to his sanity. At that moment, his wedding seemed like lightyears away and he just wanted Cheryl to walk in the door with a big smile and say, "She's okay."

Suddenly, the door opened and people began to file in. Cheryl was the first, then a police officer, two doctors, and a man in a suit. Cheryl's face was tearstained and the rest of the group looked very somber as well.

One of the doctors walked forward and introduced himself to the family members. "Hello, I'm Dr. Wilson. I'm the head administrator of the hospital. I know this has be a horrific day for everyone and especially the families of the injured. Disasters like this are very difficult and devastating to everyone involved. We've tried our best to get everything under control in an expedient manner. We are very proud of our triage colleagues. When our community is hit with a disaster like this, our job is to save every life we can and to immediately administer lifesaving medical care to all the injuries, no matter how small. Sometimes, no matter what we do, it's not enough."

Camilla, Leona, Hilary, and Austin stood there in shock, trying to read between the doctor's words and what his little speech was leading up to. Austin was crippled with a gut-wrenching feeling that Harper was lying in a hospital bed with life-threatening injuries. The visualization was overpowering and his mind was spinning in a thousand directions. The only words he had never expected to ever hear in his lifetime were softly spoken through the lips of Dr. Wilson.

"I'm really sorry to have to tell you this, but Harper was in the wrong place at the wrong time. No matter how hard we tried to save her...her injuries were too severe to sustain her life. By the time we received her in this hospital, she had already lost too much blood due to internal injuries. I'm so sorry. She passed on after every effort was made to save her."

Camilla started screaming in horror of his words. She kept screaming and crying out, "Not my daughter, not Harper...how could God do this to us? No...no...no...."

Her daughter had died and everything in her was shutting down. All four of them were stunned beyond comprehension. Hilary grabbed her mother and pulled her close to her chest in hopes of absorbing some of her pain and grief. Leona joined that small circle of pain, tears, and disbelief. This 'moment of impact' shook them to the very core of their lives—like a rag doll gripped in the mouth of a mad dog, who relentlessly refused to let go.

Tears slowly slipped down Austin's face as he stepped forward. "Where is she now? Is she alone?" Taking deep breaths, he wiped his face, trying to hold off his overwhelming need to purge his stomach. He wanted to hold her and let her know she was going to be okay. That her only dream in life was not going to be taken away. That they were going to get married and she was going to wear her mother's wedding gown. That they were going to live happily ever after....

Dr. Wilson cleared his throat, but nobody reacted. They were all lost in the horror that left them trying to understand what had just happened. He walked over to Austin and put his arms around his shoulders, trying to comfort the young man as the other strangers watched with expressions of deep sadness. This was the third family that morning that he had to soothe and comfort after the loss of their loved one. "Austin, she's in our morgue downstairs. I'm not so sure you want to see her. Her body was pretty mangled in the collision. However, that is entirely your choice. We usually require someone to identify the person. I understood Cheryl is her best friend and a nurse, so she decided to take that burden off of the family. I've brought the attending physician, Dr. Remi, here to answer any questions." The other doctor extended a hand to Austin while the two older women stayed tucked under Hilary's arms. "The other gentleman is our hospital Chaplin, Steven Brooks. He administered Harper her last rights, but you always have your options to have your church clergyman to do that as well. Steven is here to help you decide how you would like to handle this. Please feel free to ask us for any assistance you need."

Dr. Remi quietly said, "Harper was the first one taken by ambulance from the scene. By then, we were prepared for the worst. She had multiple internal injuries after being thrown around the car as it crashed into the locomotive and then derailed, rolling over many times. When we found her, she had lost forty percent of her blood. We immediately started replacing the lost blood, but the broken bones and collapsed lungs made it difficult. I don't think you want to know any more. Please accept my heartfelt condolences."

The police officer stepped forward. "I was one of the first responders on the scene within two minutes after the crash. We know the first two cars took the brunt of the collision. They smashed into the locomotive and the other cars piled into them, causing those two cars to become airborne and fall back down and roll until they came to a stop. Most of the casualties and severely injured victims were in those first few cars. We don't know why some survived and others didn't. Your fiancé's body was wrapped around a young child who miraculously survived. We don't know anything other than she must have grabbed a hold of that nine-year-old boy and held on tight to protect him. He's in critical condition, but still alive." He looked down at his shaking hand. "I'm so sorry about your family's loss. I know while I was with her for those few seconds, she whispered, 'tell them I love them.' As a nurse, I think she must have known."

Hilary was shaking, Camilla and Leona were sobbing. Austin stepped forward, silent tracks of tears running down his face. "I don't want her to be alone." He looked at Hilary and said, "You and I will make the arrangements. I want the funeral on Saturday...."

Camilla yelped, "You can't have it on your wedding day!"

Every set of eyes immediately went to Austin in shock. With his heart pounding out of his chest, his hands shaking, he responded. "Everyone has that day put aside...it's the best for now. The church is already reserved." He looked at Dr. Wilson.

"Will you please take me to Harper? I don't want her to be alone." Austin followed the doctor out of the room.

Austin was finally ushered into a small room. He sat down on the only chair. The room was extremely cold and the lights were dimmed. A nurse dressed in scrubs wheeled in the gurney with Harper's body on it. Her body was covered with a clean, crisp sheet.

The nurse asked Austin, "Would you like me to take down the sheet or would you prefer to do it? We tried to clean her up the best we could. I'm so sorry about your loss."

He shook his head. "I just want to sit and talk to her. There's a lot I have to say and I just didn't want her to be alone."

She nodded. "As soon as the arrangements are made to pick her up, things will get easier. They'll take care of everything."

Austin looked at the nurse. He knew she didn't really mean to insult him with the 'easier' remark, but anger was beginning to well up within him. He said in a soft voice, "Nothing about this is easy. Everything about this is fucking hard." Tears were running down his cheeks. "We were supposed to be married on Saturday and now instead of a wedding, our families are planning a funeral. And...I just lost my best friend."

The nurse sucked in a deep breath and said gently, "If you would like, I will sit here with you. Or if you need anything, just let me know, I will be right outside the door."

"I need her back, can you help me with that?"

"No, I'm very sorry...." She closed the door behind her.

Austin pulled the chair next to the gurney. Before he sat down, he slowly pulled down the sheet from her face. Her eyes were closed and she was bruised and beat up. But she looked peaceful. There was that familiar smile on her face that she always had when she was happy. He closed his eyes tightly and began to talk to her. He let her know how much he loved her and how proud he was that she had saved a child's life. He laughed about their morning together and how he wished now he had made wild and crazy love to her. For the next six hours, he talked about their joyous times together and how excited he had been to marry her. He knew her dream was to walk down the aisle in her mother's wedding gown, to marry her prince, and now she was laying here stone cold, gone. Gone forever.

*Where was the fairness in life? Why her?* he kept asking himself, as if there would ever be an answer.

His phone rang and he refused to answer it. He didn't want anything to disturb his last moments with his beloved lady. He wanted every second all to himself. He was glad that his mother, Camilla, and Hilary would not see this once beautiful young woman in the hollowness of death. He wanted her remembered as that sassy, bright, and beautiful nymph who had stolen his heart that evening in the hospital. Oh, God, he wanted her back.

Five days passed in a blur. Family and friends gathered together and tried to keep everything as private and quiet as possible. It was impossible to keep the funeral away from the public's eye, though, with the paparazzi hounding and snapping pictures of every move the family made. With a tragedy as over-sensationalized as the train crash, everyone wanted a piece of the grieving families. Condolence cards from strangers from around the world were pouring in, along with flowers and anything people felt the need to send. It was all meant in a positive manner, but instead it was becoming overwhelming.

True to his word, Austin personally made each call to the invited guest of the wedding to inform them that the service was going to be at the same time and the same morning as their wedding date. Hilary, who had tried her best to keep it together and not fall apart, had managed to help Austin with all the arrangements, starting at the church. Although she had some concerns about his plans and why he was doing it, she understood his convictions. Camilla and Nico were grieving too deeply to coherently participate in anything. To outlive your daughter, for her to be taken away when her life was just blossoming, was more than they could handle. Friends and family tried their best to be consoling, but they just wanted to be left alone to absorb and try to understand why this had happened.

Austin didn't want them to worry about anything. He took everything upon his own shoulders. He knew his grieving would really commence when everything he needed to get done...got done.

Leona possessed more strength than Austin had thought possible. She helped with the planning. The family gathering, after the service, was going to be held at her house. She didn't want Camilla and Nico saddled with the memories of their daughter's funeral along with a houseful of guests to commiserate their unfortunate loss. She had the caterer arrange to bring the food to her home and everyone pitched in to make sure it was a quiet but happy farewell to a beautiful life. It was going to be difficult, but it was going to be special. The priest at the church had finally agreed to do the service that Austin wanted and Camilla and Nico had reluctantly agreed as well.

The doors to the church were opened and mourners were beginning to walk in one at a time. Flowers were everywhere, and Harper's magnificent arrangements of colored blooms enhanced each pew. Austin didn't think there was any reason to cancel the order, seeing as Harper had spent many weeks working with the florist to finalize her favorites, and had been so excited for the arrangements. They were paid for and nothing was refundable. Even with the circumstance of death, vendors still had their contracts that they held you to.

The priest stood at the front door, blessing guests with the holy cross. Everyone was taking their seats on both sides of the church. Austin and Harper's favorite classical music was being played as the guests waited for the service. The mourners were sitting, emotionally charged, as they waited for the service to begin.

It had been publicly announced on the news that the first casualty of the crash was being laid to rest and many people began to gather outside. Onlookers and looky-loos waited behind the taped off areas. Others lined the streets in hopes of giving Harper's family and friends their heartfelt condolences. The news vans and paparazzi had showed up in full force to report Harper and Austin's heart rendering story, hoping to jack up their ratings. Although, they were trying to be respectful of the family, they were also hoping to get any kind of pictures that were valuable for their newscast and to spin drama about the death. Reporters had set up small sections of the street with the best view they could find of the small church, poised as they waited for the limousines to arrive.

No one was allowed in without the special card they had received prior to the service. Most of the guests arrived in the limousines with darkened windows and were taken to the back of the church where their privacy could be maintained. Austin didn't want Harper's funeral turned into a spectacle. Calmly and respectfully, Austin had stood on the steps to the church and requested respect for the family. Police officers and security guards were there to make sure that everything went smoothly. In a gesture of their sympathy, hundreds of neighbors, friends, and strangers placed flowers, candles, and cards along both sides of the road.

Once the church was filled with all of the invited guests, Austin went to the door and led the doctors, nurses, and first responders into the remaining seats, some left with standing room only.

Austin walked up to the podium and looked out over the sea of guests. Loss was written across all of their faces as he swept his eyes around the room. He met Hilary's eye in the front row and nodded. She was seated between her parents, her arms wrapped tightly around each one. She nodded back, then closed her eyes, her chin shaking. Toni, Hilary's girlfriend, sat on the other side of Camilla, holding the older woman's shaking hands tightly and securely in her own.

Austin blinked several times, trying to stem the tears silently flowing down his cheeks as he made eye contact with each individual he could, nodding to some and winking to others. He had to make it through this before he could give into his grief. His heart was broken; now all he could do was give Harper his final respects for the love they had shared.

The music stopped and Austin cleared his throat and said to the sorrowful crowd, "This day is for celebration. I know Harper would not want us to cry for her. We are going to celebrate what should have been the happiest day of our lives. That would make her happy. I want everything about this special day to be about my Harper. I miss her with every single cell in my body. My heart has been broken, but her spirit will live in me forever.... I've selected a few of her favorite songs, so sit back and remember all those wonderful moments she shared with us, and how lucky we were to have such an amazing lady in our lives."

The first song was *Hallelujah*, then *Somewhere Over the Rainbow*, *I Can't Help Falling in Love With You*, and a few more of their favorites. After the final song ended, there was quiet and all was still. Catching everyone by surprise, a piano from the balcony began to play *All of Me*, the song that was going to be performed by Deborah, a dear friend, as Harper walked down the aisle. Deborah held onto the balcony railing, singing the sweet song, choking up every now and then.

The back doors opened and very slowly the open casket was wheeled down the aisle. Harper was dressed in her mother's wedding gown and was holding the special bouquet she had ordered. The mortuary had done an amazing job with the makeup, because Harper looked peaceful, beautiful, and happy. The simple smile on her face brought everyone to tears as they all began to understand what was going to happen. The groomsmen were dressed in their white tuxedos on one side of the casket and the bridesmaids in their pastel rose dresses on the other. Cheryl, the maid of honor, and Thomas, Austin's best man, solemnly led the way in front, dropping rose petals and smiling gently at the hushed audience. Austin stood at the front with the Priest, waiting for his beautiful bride. In his hand was a microphone.

When the casket finally made it to the front, not a dry eye remained in the church. Some were sobbing, others understood where Austin was coming from. You could see the acknowledgment on their faces. What should have been a day of festivities had become a day of remembrance, honor, and mourning.

When the song stopped, Austin stepped forward. "Thank you for being part of this joyful yet sad occasion. All my Harper ever wanted in life was to walk down the aisle in her mother's wedding dress and to live happily ever after in my arms. I can't give her back her life, but I can give her the wedding she wanted so dearly and send her on her way to happily ever after. So...please understand that this special day is for her. It is the best way, I felt in my heart, I could make her dreams finally come true."

The priest walked over and slipped his arm around Austin's shoulders and whispered something in his ear. Austin turned and hugged him and then the priest handed Austin a ring.

Austin took the ring and kissed it, then bent over to place it on Harper's finger. The priest turned around and put a ring on Austin's finger, and said, "In the eyes of all these witnesses, let us acknowledge the everlasting love of my two favorite people, Austin Lewis and Harper Puzzio."

Austin bent down and kissed Harper's lips, and said, "I will love you forever...."

Almost on the verge of losing it, Thomas walked over and gave his friend a big bear hug.

Cheryl bent down and kissed her best friend goodbye and said, "You look so beautiful. I will truly miss you."

Knowing that Austin had done his best to handle what he felt was right and what Harper deserved, Thomas took the microphone, and said, "In front of you, tucked into the pews, are small cards and pencils. Please write a small note and tuck it in the casket as a special way of expressing your love for Harper."

Simultaneously, everyone bent forward and found what they were looking for. As they finished their task, they slowly formed a line to say their goodbyes and to leave their special note. Some people pinched off flowers from the arrangements on the pews and slipped them in around Harper, while others stood there, lingering, not wanting to leave. During the whole procession, Austin stood on the other side of the casket and held Harper's hand.

Austin cleared his voice and spoke up again, "In lieu of flowers, please make a donation in the back of the room for the 3rd Street mission where Harper and I spent many evenings feeding the homeless. She would appreciate that and so would I. A small reception will be held at my mother's house. Please pick up directions on the small cards at the front of the church. I personally want to thank each and every one of you for being part of Harper's life. I know she loved you all. All I ask, and I am begging you on behalf the grieving families, please do not share any photos taken today with the press or anyone you cannot trust. If I do find that you have, I will personally take action against you. I'm sorry I have to say this, but it's painful enough to have lost our loved one. To see her picture plastered across a tabloid would be sheer devastation. I want to remind everyone that only the immediate family and the wedding party are invited to the graveside service. Thank you so much."

Austin waited until everyone had said their piece and walked out the back doors to leave before he broke down. While holding onto Harper's hand, just the thought of letting go was taking him into a dark place.... A place where one single moment in time had robbed him of a lifetime of happiness. The light she had brought for the past few years was no longer going to shine. Lonely nights of never-ending memories were going to crush his spirit. They had been meant for each other and now one truck stuck on the tracks had taken her from him. *How was he going to make it through the darkness?*

Just the immediate family remained in the church to watch Austin break into a million little pieces. Camilla and Nico had not left their pew. Their grief was incapacitating. Everyone tried, but nobody could take away the agony of losing their child. They had said their goodbyes in the family's viewing room before the service. Austin could tell by the expression on Camilla's face that she would never be the same. Viewing her daughter in the wedding dress that had brought her thirty-five years of happiness with Nico was more than she could handle. It took every bit of Hilary and Nico's strength to hold her up. And yet Austin could see that, Nico too, was dying inside.

Hilary held fast to her parents. Her anger spilled over as she whispered, *"What was our mother's god thinking when he put you on that train?"* Hilary began to shake. *You were my best friend. Why did you leave me? What am I going to do without you? You were supposed to have the children and live the fairy tale. Now you abandon me here to hold up a burden I may not be able to live up to.*

Camilla's sobs could be heard throughout the church.

"Why you? Why not me?" Hilary whispered.

The gravesite was more difficult. As the last shovel of dirt was placed on the grave, everyone looked exhausted and lost.

Across the street from the cemetery, a small gathering of people stood quietly watching and waiting to see the family. The reporters and paparazzi were gone and all that was left was a large tribute of flowers, cards, candles, and numerous small objects that were meaningful to those who mourned for a young lady who had died too young.

The gathering across the street was comprised of one Hispanic family. Protected in the middle was an older man who was on his knees. His hands were clinched together as he prayed and sobbed and continued to rock back and forth. His wife was down on her knees, holding him tight against her body, as the man continued to cry out in pain. Four adult children surrounded him as they brokenly endured their father's grief.

He sobbed between his words. He kept whispering, *"Lo siento por su pérdida...lo siento...lo siento...."* The pain was felt through his words, bringing tears to everyone's eyes.

His wife held him closer, and said, "It was not your fault, *querido*.... The truck was stuck. You tried so hard to get it off the tracks. Everyone tried so hard. This is not your fault."

Misery seeped into his words as the guilt of the accident and the lives it stole haunted him. *"Lo siento.... Lo siento...yo siento tu el dolor!"*

One of the sons leaned down and put his hand on his father's shoulder. "Papa, this was not your fault. We did everything possible to get it off.... I even destroyed our other truck trying to push it off. They know this...." He inhaled a deep breath and exhaled slowly. "You can't put this all on your shoulders, Papa." The son stood up and hit his chest with his fist. "I will take half your blame. Don't do this...please, Papa."

The old man laid his forehead on the warm cement sidewalk and continued to wail, *"Lo siento, lo siento...."*

The family in the cemetery never looked across the street. They were filled with too much grief to notice anything....

# CHAPTER 11

## José

José opened his eyes and closed them again, just like a butterfly flutters his wings. He didn't know if he was alive or dead or if this was all a bad dream. The only thing he knew for certain was that he was in tremendous pain.

Feeling like he was floating in a cloud, faint voices and noises began to drift around him—and none of them sounded familiar. The only thing he could faintly remember was the violent tossing of his body and...pain. A twisting pain, along with the screams, kept haunting his dreams.

*Had the police caught him? Had they shot him? Was he one that they nearly beat to death?*

José went back to that feeling of floating. Nothing could hurt him there—he felt safe.

Maria had sat in the chair next to José's bed for the past week with her rosary beads, praying that her son would not die. The violence of the crash and the fact that he was in the first car left her unable to comprehend how he had survived at all. Watching the news and feeling awful for the people on the train was hard enough. When she got the call from the hospital, she had nearly passed out. To hear from a stranger that her young son was on the crashed train sent her into a wildly emotional state of fear. When the doctor came onto the phone and announced José was in critical condition, all she could do was cry, *"No es mi bebé, por favor, no mi bebé!"* Filled with fear that was about to send her over the edge, she felt her consciousness began to slowly slip away.

Within the hour she was running through the doors of the hospital in search of her son. Grasping her rosary beads in one hand and holding her chest in the other, she walked up to the information desk and handed them a piece of paper. Written on it, in the best and only knowledge of the English language she had, were the words, 'Doctur Eglum' and 'ICU.'

The young woman at the desk looked at her, slightly puzzled. "Maybe you could tell me who you spoke with? This name doesn't look familiar."

Stuttering with every word, she said, "Doctor Ingram. I don't know what the letters mean, but he say to me to let you know those three letters. He said you would tell me where my son is. Please, tell me, please." Her tears were starting to run down her cheeks. Maria's English was broken, but not enough that it was incomprehensible. Some of her verbs were a little off because she had never attended school past the third grade and her grasp of the English language had been slowly picked up through the years.

The young lady nodded. She took out a stack of papers and shifted through them.

"Okay, I will try to explain this the best I can. I will also write it down. If you get lost or confused, someone upstairs will help you out." She wrote down instructions on a sheet of paper and handed it to Maria. "I need you to take the elevator up." She pointed to the hall of elevators against the back wall that were constantly opening and closing with people getting in and out. "Take it up to the fifth floor—*numero cinco*. When you get up there, go to the nurse's station. They will help you from there. Okay?"

Maria wiped her eyes. "*Si, senorita.* Thank you so much."

Immediately Maria ran over to the elevators and waited patiently for one to open with the green arrow pointing up. When it did, she shuffled inside. Still holding her breath and rubbing her beads, she rode up to the fifth floor silently and finally stepped out onto solid ground and walked over to the desk area, still grasping the piece of paper she had scribbled the information on.

There were nurses and doctors everywhere—coming and going. One nurse at the desk was sitting at the computer typing on the keyboard. Maria waited without complaint for the nurse to look up and acknowledge her.

When she finally did, the nurse said, "I'm sorry, it's been crazy around here. You should have caught my attention." She smiled sweetly. "How can I help you? Are you looking for someone?"

Maria nodded her head.

"What's their name?"

"José Rafael Joaquin Rodriguez," Maria said, handing her the scribbled note.

The nurse smiled as she looked on the screen of her computer. "Okay, I found him. We only have José Rodriquez."

Maria slightly grinned. "Yes, that is my son."

The nurse leaned forward on her chair and a more serious look crossed her face. "Has anyone talked with you or told you of his injuries?"

"No...."

The nurse stood up and approached Maria with great care. "Have a seat for just one moment as I find the doctor who is treating him. *Uno momento, por favor.*"

Within a few minutes a young doctor was standing in front of her. He extended his hand and said, "I'm Dr. Lee Ong."

She extended her hand. "I'm Maria Loretta Sanchez Rodriguez. José is my son."

He took her hand and walked her over to two chairs across from the nurse's desk. "Have a seat," he said in a soft-spoken voice as he took the other seat. "Your son was severely injured. José was in the first car that was almost completely demolished. I can only say that I'm so proud of our fast and efficient triage doctors, because without their quick medical attention, José would not be here. He is in critical condition, but we are all hopeful. The next forty-eight hours are very critical and they will determine if he makes it or not."

Maria placed her hands over her face and began to cry. The doctor leaned over and put his arms around her shoulders as her heartrending sobs filled the room. After a few minutes, he lifted her chin and looked directly at her. "I want you to know that because he is young, he has a better chance than most. I'm really banking money that he will pull through."

"You have money in the bank to get him through? I don't understand...."

Dr. Ong grinned. "That's just a figure of speech. It was...."

Her face showed confusion as her tears began to flow again.

"I meant...I think he will be okay. He might have to spend a while here in the hospital until we can get him back to where he was. But I want you to know that the doctors and staff are working really hard to make sure he pulls through. Okay?"

Between her small sobs, she whispered, "What kind of hurt? Did he lose anything?"

"No, he has a lot of internal injuries and many broken bones. He still has his arms and legs. He is pretty beaten up and will be almost unrecognizable to you and the family. I want you to know that we put him into an induced coma so his body could heal with less stress. Don't be afraid when you see all the tubes and machines attached to him. All of it has gotten him to this point, and it just looks scary."

Maria stood up and held her chest. She looked at the doctor and said, "We have no medical insurance. We have nothing, so how will I pay for this?"

He stood up and put his arm around her shoulder. "That should not be a worry right now. I'm sure everything will be picked up by the state. I don't want you or José to worry about that or anything at all...I just want him back to the way he was before the crash."

She touched the doctor's sleeve, and said, "Can I see *mi hijo*?"

With concerned eyes, he said, "Absolutely. We set up a bed in there so you could stay however long you want." Dr. Lee Ong was a compassionate doctor and it showed on his face. He was of a smaller stature and of Asian descent and could not have been older than thirty-five. Maria looked at him as though he was a giant of a man by the way he was sympathetically protecting her.

"*Gracias*, Dr. Ong. You have been so kind." A look of surprise crossed her face when he gently took her hand and walked her down the ICU ward towards her son's room.

He stopped at a door and turned towards her. "Like I said, we are waiting for him to pull through, and he doesn't look too good. I will be in every hour, along with other doctors and nurses. Okay? And...we don't want any visitors other than you, right now, okay?"

Maria was humbled and nodded.

When they walked through the door, her world began to spin again as a dizzy feeling threatened to knock her off of her feet. There were tubes coming from every part of his body. Loud machines and monitors were strategically placed around the room. The rhythmic sound of the ventilator pumping the air in and out of his lungs was loud in her ears. His face was twice its size and he was unrecognizable. She took in a deep breath and held it until she walked around the bed to his side. Then she exhaled and sat on the chair the doctor had moved next to the bed for her to sit on.

She stared at her baby as a new wave of tears overwhelmed her. Again, Dr. Ong showed tremendous sympathy and handed her a box of tissues.

He said, "You can pick up his hand very carefully. You can talk to him even though he's in a coma. We don't know if he will hear it, but it might make you feel better."

Maria looked at the doctor with sad eyes reflected her pain, and then slowly and carefully picked up José's hand and began to whisper in Spanish to him.

For six days Maria sat in the room holding his hand, mumbling words a mother would say to her son in hopes he could hear her. The first few days it was touch and go, and one evening many of the machines had started ear-piercing shrills. Immediately, the room filled with nurses and doctors. After what seemed like an eternity, they all released deep sighs of relief, knowing they had gotten him through a major crisis that almost took his life.

Early in the morning on the sixth day, Dr. Ong came into the room. He stood next to Maria and said, "I'm extremely happy with his prognosis and I'm going to take him out of the induced coma. Watch him closely and let the nurses know if he shows any signs of normal movement. Things like moving his fingers or toes or blinking his eyes...anything," he explained.

"*Gracias*...I appreciate all you have done. I don't know how to repay everyone."

"Live a good life—that is all I ask of José and you...."

"He's young...I have cancer and will not be here long."

His eyes opened wide. "What kind of cancer?"

Maria looked down toward the floor and told him her story, of how she couldn't find a doctor to help and her struggles without insurance. She knew José was worried about her and had tried all he could, but nobody helped or cared. "All I want now is my baby to make something out of his life. I don't want him to die in the *barrio* like his brother.

I've tried my best as a single mother, but life hasn't been fair." She never looked up. "He's a good boy and wants to go to college."

Dr. Ong listened to her wretched story. His eyes narrowed and the expression on his face turned to anger. "Our healthcare system is broken in this country and it's an embarrassment to us doctors. I'm so sorry, Maria. I'm going to look into this." He apologized profusely and then he turned, took out a needle from José's arm, placed a piece of tape over it, took the bag it was attached to, and quietly walked out of the room.

That afternoon, as Maria had done for the past week, she held José's hand and squeezed it occasionally. She always held his hand while she was talking to him or singing him his favorite childhood songs. Suddenly, she felt a slight squeeze back. She squeezed again, only harder, and looked disappointed that she didn't feel him squeeze back.

Letting out a deep breath, she thought to herself, *Me pregunto si podría haber sido un reflejo de algún tipo o tal vez sólo mi imaginación,* asking if it had been a reflex or just her imagination.

Unexpectedly, he squeezed her hand again, only this time harder. Panic and excitement began to show on her face as she watched him also flutter his eyes open and then closed.

Maria jumped up from the seat and began to hit the button for the nurses. Her thumb continued to press down hard as her elation and excitement could be heard throughout the room. She screamed his name over and over, looking for him to open his eyes once again. Within seconds, a few of the night nurses came charging through the door.

Not sure what could have set off all the commotion, the head nurse, Stella, said, "Are you okay, Maria? What is going on?"

Maria was so excited, she screamed, "¡*Querido, él me apretó la mano!*"

A big grin lit up Stella's face. She nodded her head and walked toward the bed with anticipation. The young nurse with Stella asked, "What is she saying, Stella?"

Stella smiled broadly and translated. "He squeezed her hand."

Stella was slowly walking around the bed, checking certain vital signs, when she noticed his eyes were slightly open and following her movement. The thin slit was almost a squint, but it was enough to see his dark brown eyes and she sighed. "Well, it looks like we are definitely into recovery mode. Looks like this young man has decided to join us. I'm going to call Dr. Ong...."

Maria was on her knees next to the bed, rejoicing, rolling her rosary beads over and over in her hands and praying as quickly as she could. Her voice was soft and the nurses noticed the tears streaming down her cheeks.

Stella walked over and helped her up before she walked out the door. "You did a great job, but now we need you to talk to José and see if we can coach him out of his coma further."

"*Si!*"

José's eyes fluttered open when he heard his mother's voice. A slight grin crossed his face as the corner of his lips gradually arched upward. Most of the swelling on his face had gone down and his bruises were now that awkward yellowish color, making him appear jaundiced. His eyes made contact with his mother and then they sluggishly closed again.

After the next few hours, he fell back to sleep and woke up again for a few more minutes. This time a little more lucid. And for the next few days, his recovery was measured and producing progressive results. Dr. Ong had determined there were no neurological injuries from all the trauma his head sustained during the violent derailment, but José still had yet to speak a word.

On the third day after he came out of his coma, in a quiet whisper, José asked his mother, "Where is Angel? I have not seen him." It was the first time he had actually talked. He had only been nodding his head slightly for 'yes' and 'no' answers.

Sadness crossed Maria's face and she looked away. "He's in jail. They picked him up the day of the crash. He had some warrants out for his arrest. They don't know when he will get out. The public defender is working on the case."

"Has he called you?"

"*Si*. He calls once a day to see how you are doing, *hijo*. He's been so worried."

José sighed and closed his eyes. The look of relief on his face was not noticed by Maria. She was too busy straightening up the bed and making sure her baby was okay.

José, on the other hand, was thinking to himself, *Thank God Angel's not here. I could not go through a major blowout with him right now over the stupid thing I did or where the gun was.* The gun was lost in the crash. *Will that really matter?* he asked himself. *I'm sure someone saw me get onto the train. The police are probably waiting for me to get better so they can interrogate and arrest me. Maybe I should just kept sleeping.* His final thought was of his mother before he drifted off to sleep. *If I get arrested, it is going to kill madre.* A tear slipped out from the corner of his eye.

Days later, and there was still no law enforcement or anyone at the hospital to arrest him. He couldn't understand why, nor did he want to say anything. There were a few NTSB inspectors that had a few questions, but nothing which he could answer; he didn't have any extra information that would help. Everything had happened so quickly that nobody had even one acknowledgeable second to prepare for the crash, no warning so that they could brace themselves for the impact. He did hear the loud horn blowing, but he had thought it was just to let an approaching stop know of the train. Or, to try to give notice to the children who were constantly playing on the tracks in that area.

Diego came once to see José, but Maria sent him on his way when he started to tease and irritate José about his brother. Diego said, as he pranced around the room, "Hey, what happened to the piece? Did you use it or lose it?" He started to laugh. "Oh, I like that rhyme."

José's eyes opened wide and he whispered, "Get the fuck out of here, you twerp!"

Maria saw how upset José was and politely asked Diego to leave. On his way out the door, he turned to José and asked again, "Did you use it or lose it?"

José knew exactly what he was saying, only didn't dare say a word. Diego had a big mouth, and now that Angel was in jail, he could spout it off without the fear of retaliation. More importantly, José's fear

161

that his mother would find out he was 'packing a piece' was making him feel sick.

On sleepless nights at the hospital, he would obsess about the whereabouts of the gun. Finally, one day a NTSB agent and a police officer came into his room again to ask questions about a gun they had found in the wreckage of the train car. He didn't acknowledge that it was his. He just looked at them with innocent eyes that left them believing he didn't know anything about it. After they walked out of the room, José laid his head back against his pillows with a weary sigh and closed his eyes. At least the mystery of the whereabouts of the gun was over. There was nothing to track it to him or Angel. Now all he had to worry about was the chance he might be identified on the pharmacy's cameras.

While José was lying down, resting, the dim light shining above the bed, his door opened. Thinking it was just another nurse or doctor, José pretended to be asleep. The soft tapping of leather shoes walking on the tile floor had him laying perfectly still. The footsteps stopped at the foot of his bed, and then he heard a male voice. The man cleared his throat and said, "José, I would like to talk to you."

The man pulled up the only chair in the room next to the front of the bed. Maria had gone home for the night so the empty and quiet room was almost unnerving to José.

Unfamiliar with the voice and not sure what to do, José opened his eyes and looked at the man sitting at the foot of his bed. "Do I know you?" José quietly asked.

The man grinned. "I'm not sure. You were a terribly frightened young man the last time I saw you. In fact, the last time I saw you, I had a lot of cleaning up to do. Do you remember me?"

José knew exactly who he was, but he was not going to let on. He was too frightened to give any information away to this stranger so he could use it against him. "No, should I?"

The pharmacist stood up and smiled. "My name is Assandro Garcia, and you know exactly who I am. I can see it in your eyes. You are just as frightened now as you were that day." He inched closer. "I know you got on that train."

José didn't say anything. He was not only caught, but this man could seal the destiny of his young life and send him to prison for armed theft. After a few silent and charged minutes, José's shoulders drooped and he covered his face with a shaky hand, pressing his fingers against his closed eyes. His voice was hollow as he admitted the truth. "I didn't mean for the gun to go off. I didn't want to hurt anyone. I just wanted those medications for *mi madre*. I love my mother and to watch her die a slow death forced me to make the stupidest decision of my life...." His hand fell to his side on the bed and he met Assandro's eyes respectfully. "I'm sorry."

"I am going to disclose a few things to you, and if you ever say anything to anyone, I will deny everything...*entendido*?"

José nodded his head. He understood. He tried to sit up and get comfortable. He didn't want to call the nurse, but he needed help. Assandro saw him struggling, so he helped him sit up without a fuss. After José was settled, Assandro swung the chair around. "I knew you were pressured into doing what you did because of the pain of losing your mother to cancer. I understand that. I lost my mother to cancer. But I was able to take

163

her to the best hospitals and doctors money could buy. Your story at the counter about not receiving any help from our broken healthcare system is something I hear on a regular basis. However, the way you went about it is not going to do your mother any good, nor will it get her what she needs. It will only have you serving ten years in jail, missing the last months of her life." Assandro raised one eyebrow as he eyed José squarely. "*Hombre joven*, was it worth it?"

José's heart was beating out of his chest. Tears were beginning to well and with the sleeve of his pajamas, he wiped them away. Slowly, he shook his head.

Satisfied, Assandro nodded. "I wiped the counters before the police could look for fingerprints. When the police asked for the film from our camera system, I accidentally exposed the film and nothing could be recovered. The only thing I could not retrieve was the bullet or the gun. The witnesses only described you as a young man in a hoodie. I just said your face was too shadowed to make out any distinguishing features. I guess you could say...I covered your ass."

José's eyes were wide with disbelief. "Why?"

Assandro looked down at his clasped hands and then looked back up. "I knew what you were doing was not really criminal. You just didn't know how or where to find help for your mother. I've never aided and abetted anyone in my life for a criminal act, but I thought God would protect me on this one."

José shook his head, bewildered and humbled. "They came in yesterday to ask about the gun they found in the train. I don't think they connected it to the attempted robbery. My brother etched off the numbers when he gave it to me and...I wiped it down just before the crash." José looked repentant. "I told them it was not mine."

"Then there is no way they can trace it to you." Assandro leaned forward and said, "You're getting a second chance. I don't want you to blow this one! We are going to keep this little secret between us."

"Okay." Jose closed his eyes and leaned into his pillows, a great tide of relief allowing him to truly relax for the first time since he had awoken from his coma and remembered the mess he had made. "Thank you."

Assandro took out several folded papers from his jacket pocket and handed them to José. "I want your mother to fill out these papers the best she can. I will stop by tomorrow to pick them up. I made a few phone calls to UCLA's medical center and they are going to take your mother as a patient on a *pro gratis* basis."

José looked confused. "What does *pro gratis* mean?"

Assandro smiled. "It means they will treat your mother's cancer and pay for all medications and anything else she may need. Occasionally, they take on 'charity' cases and I just happen to know the head of oncology, so he's willing to do that for you." Assandro drew his brows together and looked stern. "No more shenanigans...and I want you to check in with me every week and let me know how everything is going. Promise to behave?"

José, wide-eyed and emotionally shaken, meekly and firmly nodded his head and then turned his head into his pillow and began to sob. Assandro stood and placed a hand on his shoulder. "I know what it is like to live in the *barrio* and to lose the only thing you have left." He watched as José wiped his face with his sheet, and then he said, "There was a reason why you walked into my pharmacy that day. There was some kind of divine intervention that put you on that train and this 'moment of impact' has changed your life forever."

José grasped his hand and said, "Thank you so much. My mother thanks you, and I'm forever grateful."

Assandro ruffled the young boy's head and smiled, and then he walked toward the door and turned around. "Tomorrow. I will pick those papers up tomorrow, and hopefully by Monday we can start getting your mother the care that she so desperately needs."

José watched Assandro, tears streaming down his face, and nodded.


Maria Rodriguez had not slept well the night before and she was exhausted by the time she had taken the three buses to the hospital. She still did not know what José had done. He told her he had taken the train to get some art supplies in the city and she believed him. He never lied to her. Not like her other sons. She was starting to cramp up and she sat in the lobby so José could not see her distress. When the pills finally eased her pain, she got off the lobby chair and went to his room.

José was sitting up in his bed. A big smile spread across his face when his mother walked in. He couldn't wait to tell her the good news. He waved the papers in his hand around like a flag.

Maria smiled and asked, "What's all this excitement about? Did you win the lotto? I bet you asked that pretty nurse out for a date? No?"

"I wish, Mama. I have some unbelievable news. This pharmacist that I talked to the other day has made a promise to help you get medical treatment. I told him how horribly we had been treated, and when he saw me on the news, he stopped by. He was really nice and said he had talked to some special doctors at UCLA and they are going to see you for free!'

"What, *hijo*? You're talking crazy. Nobody is going to help me."

He started to move around in bed. "We need to fill out these papers for him so he can get you in immediately for treatment. Honestly, Mama. He's going to help us."

"Who is this man? What does he want?"

"To help us, Mama!"

The door opened and Angel walked in. José and Maria froze in shock. José leaned back in bed, a little wary, hoping his brother knew nothing about what he had done and wouldn't ask for his gun back.

"How did you get out of jail?" José asked.

Angel walked toward the bed and laughed. "Looks like I have ten lives instead of nine! They couldn't find their paperwork so they had to let me go. No doubt they will find it and I will be back in the slammer, but for now, I get to visit my one-hell-of-a-lucky brother who beat the odds."

José looked nervous. "Beat the odds?"

He clipped his brother on the head and said, "Yes, *hijo*...you survived the crash and I bet you can sue and make a bundle."

"I don't care about suing them. I'm excited, because this wonderful pharmacist I stopped in to visit the other day is having Mama fill out forms and he is personally taking her to the oncology department at

UCLA to start tests and get her started on medications." He waved the forms in the air. "See!"

Shock registered all over Angel's face. "Wow...you did it, little brother! I'm proud of you, *hijo!*"

José smiled. "He is coming today to get the paperwork and she is going at the end of the week. He made me a promise."

Angel leaned over his brother and gave him a big bear hug. "You take care of her. She needs you and you need her. You are my brave bro."

José beamed with pride. He also smiled because he knew that his brother would never know the true story....

# CHAPTER 12

## Karyn

Karyn was looking out the window from her hospital bed and could see all of the tall buildings in the distance. Pedestrians were walking in all directions. Life had gone on, in spite of the fatal train crash that had taken the lives of twenty-one people and given Karyn a near-death experience. In that one moment in time, so many lives were changed, like the ripples undulating through the surface of the water after a pebble has been dropped. Karyn wondered if she would have a job or custody of her children when she got out of the hospital. The constant worry for the past few weeks was making her insides knot up and causing her MS to flair. But then again, worrying about her future had always been a constant in her life.

Karyn was trying to concentrate on the view and the loud beeping of the monitor instead of what the lady was about to tell her. She had been through this too many times. When Child Services had sent someone out to her house, each time it was someone new. The only thing they all had in common was that none of them really cared about her—or her problems. They just had to document their case report, and just as quickly, move to the next assignment.

Karyn inhaled a deep breath and let it out slowly. Her thoughts were turning in every direction and she could not think clearly. *Why is this happening to me? What did I do to deserve this? Why didn't I just die on the train? Someone please put me out of this misery!* She sighed loudly. *I don't complain or bother anyone. I just scrap together what little life has to offer me and my children. Hell, I'm just trying to survive without sinking into a dark hole.* She turned her head toward the lady sitting on the chair.

Emily Blake cleared her throat to get Karyn's attention. She was watching Karyn look out the window with an expression of desperation carved across her face. Emily extended her hand to the young woman. Karyn didn't make any attempt to accept her peace offering. Nonplussed, Emily continued talking. "I was assigned to your case a few days ago, so I've been going over all of your files. I came here to see how you were doing and how I could assist with this terrible nightmare you've been going through. I'm so sorry." She took a deep breath and continued, "I'm sure it's overwhelming and we are going to try our best to get you back home and situated with the least amount of worry."

Just a few years back, Emily Blake was barely out of her undergraduate program in sociology and was desperately trying to determine which direction in life she should take. She knew that she didn't want to be like her siblings and take over the family corporation that had been handed down from generation to generation. She wanted more out of life. Dealing with finance was meaningless to her, and continuing the affluent lifestyle was becoming more and more empty and frivolous.

One night after helping hand out hot dinners to the small children in the nearby homeless shelter, Emily eagerly made her final decision. That first night with those children was an eye-opener that left its indelible mark. One simple moment of impact and she knew exactly where she was going in life, in spite of her family's disapproval. Within two years she had pushed her way through graduate school. After graduation, she sought a position within the government's social service department and for the past two years she had interned in many family crisis centers and children's centers. She found the work to be very gratifying, but for some reason, it wasn't enough. She wanted to help change the system and give to those in need. Every day, families were torn apart and their children were forced to live in the smoldering ruins of what should have been every child's metaphorical castle, a happy home. Worse still, there were so many children who had no bed to sleep in or food to satisfy their gnawing bellies. Her sensitive heart was burdened by the weariness and pain of parents who fought against the backbreaking odds and silently wept as they watched their children suffer the storm of poverty.

Emily was an inexhaustible dreamer with a big heart for those less fortunate. Never in her younger years had she been subjected to extreme poverty and what it looked like from the inside looking out. She tried to absorb and comprehend the difference in the societal standards that gave to the rich, but took from the poor—it just didn't make sense to her anymore. The anxiety while walking down those streets and the desperation on the faces of some of those small children she encountered haunted her for months. The walk had created a passionate calling in her life.

Emily Blank went to one of the best Universities in the country. Just out of college, she accepted a job with Children's Services in Los Angeles, and was excited to accumulate experience in the field she valued. As a social worker she was able to see a desperate part of everyday life that left her disillusioned. Families and children were torn apart by a system that was not working, sometimes leaving her feeling helpless.

Emily had come from an affluent family who had hopes of her one day taking over the family's manufacturing business—it was a given for the overachievers that her parents produced. They wanted her to be in a secure place where she could find comfort and wealth, not as a social worker with long hours and little pay.

Emily wasn't looking for a financially lucrative job. She did not let the size of a paycheck dictate the kind of occupation she went into. She had seen that too many times with her family and friends. What was important to her was the emotional and rewarding feeling she got when she helped others in an unjustified world of 'haves and have nots.' Unfortunately, with the shrinking budget in California, and fewer social workers, the caseloads had become overwhelming. It was hard when she had to spread herself so thin between her cases. She wanted to do the best she could, but with the growing number of cases, it had become nearly unmanageable. She had learned to focus on the most important factor of each case and worked hard to find a suitable resolution.

Emily had spent the past few evenings reading pages and pages of transcripts from this new case. It was a sad scenario of a struggling single mother and her two children. If it wasn't bad enough that Karyn was suffering from MS, her son was headed down the wrong path in life and there wasn't a father or family member she could depend on—there was no one. Not a single person had helped this young mother through any of her struggles. She was barely keeping her head above water and now she had found herself in the middle of one of the worst train crashes in history. Emily didn't know what road this case was heading down, or how it was going to impact this family. She knew they needed assistance, and as quickly as possible.

Karyn listened to her caseworker's introduction and finally turned her head towards Emily. She said, "Do you think that you can just waltz in here and 'get me back home' so we can all pretend everything is hunky dory? If you read my files, you know the spoils of my life." Karyn turned back toward the window.

Emily scooted her chair closer to the bed. "That's why I'm here. I want to find a way to help. I honestly do want to get you back home." She looked down at her notes. "I see here that your daughter is staying at a temporary foster home while you're recovering. After I leave here, I'm going to visit her to see how she is doing. I've been talking with your doctors to see what your prognosis is and how long you may need to be hospitalized."

This time Karyn swung around with narrowed eyes. Frustrated tears spilled over and she refused to wipe them away or acknowledge them at all in front of this stranger. "Go home. At least *you* have a home to go *to*. I've been in the hospital for two weeks and I'm sure my landlord has already locked me out of the house and I'll have nothing to go back to. Don't you get it?" She sighed. "I've lost everything—again. I don't even get to salvage one pair of underwear to change into. They lock you out and everything you have becomes nothing but trash to them!" Karyn curled up as much as she could and began to quietly sob, closing her eyes tight, and willing the woman to go away.

Emily stood up and placed her hand on Karyn's back. Karyn flinched and tried to move away. Emily nodded, but kept her stance. "I've already been to your landlord. I had the state issue a check for the next few months while you're in the hospital. You're not going to lose a thing. The state is going to keep you afloat until you're back on your feet."

Karyn gradually turned around, blinking several times, not sure if she could believe such news. Finally, she asked, "...what about my job? What good is a home if you don't have a job to pay for it?"

Emily patted her hand. "Your boss is keeping it open. He knows how hard you've struggled and this whole fiasco was out of your control." Emily bent forward and made direct eye contact. "I'm really not your enemy. I really do want to help. I want to see you well, with your daughter in your care, and for your son to come back home. I've read enough in your chart to know you have been struggling for a long time. I want to see if I can get him in with a special friend of mine who deals with this sort of disruptive behavior. I'm sure she will be able to find out why he's so angry."

Karyn whispered, *"Why...?* It doesn't take a genius to know why he's so angry. And why, may I ask, after all these years, does the state have an interest in me? Are they afraid I might bring a lawsuit against the Metrorail? *...why are you here?"*

Emily whispered back, "Why not...?" She stood up straight and looked down at the young mother in the hospital bed with expressive eyes. "I have lots to do! I want you to just relax and get better while I begin to arrange things in the next few days. I don't want you to worry about your house, your job, or your children...just consider this a mini-vacation."

Karyn closed her eyes. *It has been years since anyone gave me any kind of a break. Money is scarce and life has been difficult, but no one has ever cared. For years I raised my children alone, on a salary that could only afford a broken-down trailer.*

"When can I see Penny and Kane?" Karyn asked.

"Not sure about Kane—I'm working really hard on that with my boss, but I pick up Penny tomorrow at noon and I'll bring her here for a visit. Okay?"

For the first time in weeks, Karyn weakly grinned and nodded her head as tears rolled unchecked, once again, down her cheeks.


The two nurses in the room were so excited for Karyn's daughter to visit. They spent part of the morning straightening up the room and preparing Karyn for the visit.

175

They helped her take her first real shower. They combed her hair, making it almost impossible to see the bald spot that had been shaved for needed stitches. One of the nurses dressed Karyn in a ruffled white blouse she had brought from home and carefully applied some makeup to tone down the healing scars. Karyn was looking the best she had since the accident and was sitting up in bed, waiting for Emily to bring Penny. The clock's minute hand on the wall was barely moving and she was getting antsy to see her baby. *What am I going to say to make things better for her? She's in foster care, for god's sake!*

The door flew open and Penny came running to the bed. Without hesitation, Penny jumped on top of it—bouncing everywhere. Nothing needed to be said. She was a typical eleven- year-old who didn't think or worry about any repercussions of the jumping leap as she landed next to her mother and smothered her with kisses. Tears of joy filled Karyn's eyes, but she didn't want her daughter to see them. She carefully wiped them with the sheet that rested at her waist as she watched her daughter's every movement.

Penny was filled with uncontrollable energy at the sight of her mother. A sad look crossed her face. "Mommy, I was so scared for you. I came home from school and you weren't there. I went next door and nobody knew where you were. I called your work, but they said you did not show up or call in. I thought you might have gotten lost somewhere and I cried so hard!" That sad look changed to happy as she continued her story. "Then I did what you always told me to do in case something happened to you…I called the police!" Penny put her hand over her mouth and began to giggle.

Karyn ran her hands all over her daughter's body, just to make sure she wasn't dreaming. "You did a great job, baby. I'm so glad you did call the police." Karyn lovingly smiled at her daughter as her hands cupped her small face. "I'm sorry you have to stay with strangers. I hope they're treating you well. I will be out of here soon, so we can be together again. I promise...okay?" She pulled her daughter's head toward her lips and kissed her forehead. "I miss you, baby."

Penny pulled away as she always did and then she began to gently bounce on the bed. "It's really neat at their house. We had fun playing 'twistee' yesterday. Wow, Mom, I can't believe I won! My body twisted like this...." Penny made a contorted move with her legs and arms. Then she burst out into childlike laughter.

Karyn felt like a knife was twisting in her gut, but as she continued to watch her silly little daughter, she too began to laugh. "Sounds like you're having fun. I'm so happy...."

Emily had been standing at the door. She didn't want to interrupt those first few moments between mother and daughter. She watched the love that passed through their eyes and saw for herself that Karyn was a great mother. In spite of her case records, moments like these don't appear in black and white on a piece of paper. Most social workers don't get to experience these kinds of intimate responses between child and parent. She knew, that for all that Karyn had gone through, she was a loving mother who was doing the best she could. Especially after being diagnosed with MS a few years back. Although it wasn't the best or loveliest home—she did keep a roof over the children's heads and shoes on their feet and food in their mouths—while earning only a pittance. And who knew the last time Karyn had last spent a dime just on herself?

Karyn struggled with pain daily, but got up every morning to get her children to school and go to work. Without access to a car, she diligently took the train to and from work every day without complaint, sometimes walking miles in the rain—how many mothers would do that?

This was not always the case in the families that Emily worked with. Many were so broken, the only option left to her was to break them apart—completely. It was always heartrending when Emily had to go in and tear a family apart for the sake of the children. She had dealt with all types of families that had come from different societal statuses. It didn't matter where they lived, their financial standing, or nationality--they all had one common denominator—they were all in crises. That was the hard truth of her career. But Emily was bolstered and felt a great sense of peace, because she knew that Karyn and Penny were going to be one of the lucky families to make it through the storm intact.

Karyn's case was completely different than most. Emily wasn't sure she was given the whole background and nothing made sense in the chart notes. Most of the notes were unreadable and the others painted a different picture. What little she knew was starting to fade, as she watched the mother and daughter interact with each other. They both loved each other very much, you could see it in their eyes.

*So, where is the problem? Kane?* Emily asked herself. *Where is his hostility coming from and can he be reached at his age?* Emily silently mumbled to herself, *"This is not happening on my watch...maybe I can still reach him...."*

After reading Kane's records, Emily could see how Kane had been becoming abusive toward his mother. He was lashing out at her. Normal for a teenager with all the pain he was carrying around. *But why?* Emily decided she was going to get this family out of their crisis. But first, she had to make sure Karyn was physically healthy enough to carry that heavy load on her shoulders.

With enough of her resources, she was sure to be able to finally offer some relief to the young mother. Together they would work on getting Kane into treatment, so he could channel his anger in a healthy manner and come home where he belonged.

A week had passed since Penny's first visit and the doctors saw a tremendous difference in Karyn's recovery. She was happy, distracted from her trauma, and enjoying daily visits with Penny, immensely. Having her daughter around each day gave her the stability she so desperately needed. They played cards, watched movies, and did all the normal things a daughter would do with her mother. Emily watched from a distance and drew pleasure from Karyn's transformation. She wasn't really as concerned with Penny. Kids were survivors who managed to be more resilient than adults. Karyn had a parental history of maintaining all the responsibilities without any reprieve or help. She was so beaten down there was no place to hide and nowhere to go.

That morning Emily had a big surprise. She didn't care what lines she had to sign on or how many times she crossed her t's. She was a bound and determined young woman. In her hand she held a one-day release pass for Kane to visit his mother at the hospital. The visit had to be supervised the entire time and he had to be back on time without any slip ups. It would have taken weeks to get a state-ordered aide to stay with Kane all day during the visit. Those kind of visits sometimes took months to organize because of the limited staff in the CS department. So, Emily decided she would do it herself. She put in a request to her supervisor for the one-day pass and even if she had to take a personal day off from work, this was going to happen, no matter what.

When she had gone to see Kane a few days before, he was skeptical and openly displayed his hatred for the system he was now stuck in. Emily could tell that his emotions were torn between acting out and causing this visit to be forfeited—or being more compliant and seeing his mother.

Emily took Kane for a walk. "Have a seat. Let's talk."

"What for?" His eyes narrowed as he answered her question. "So you can tell me what a fucking monster I am? Or maybe you want to tear me into shreds like everyone else does."

Emily sat for a moment without saying a word. She had seen this so many times and found her own kind of style on how to deal with these lost children. After a few silent moments, she quietly said, "Your mother almost lost her life. She's been in the hospital for weeks trying to get better so she can take your sister home and fight the system to get you back. Give me a fucking break with your piss-poor attitude. She deserves more! In fact, she deserves a big medal for lasting and surviving this far into the game. Quit feeling sorry for yourself and grow up."

Kane turned his head away. "You social workers think you know everything, but you really don't know fucking shit about me or my family or my messed up life. I get one fucking call every few days, and now that she's in the hospital, I don't know a fucking thing that is going on!"

Emily said, "Then why do you put yourself in this position?" She placed a card in his hand. "This is my card. Call me when you get angry, but please, don't blow up. Try to control your emotions. That'll make it so much easier to get you out of here."

He kept his face averted from her steady gaze. He whispered in a low voice, "Why...? I hate my life, I hate what my dad did to us, and I hate that she has MS!" His face was pained as he finally turned and made eye contact.

Emily didn't want to answer immediately. She could see that he was struggling to not show how deeply he was hurting. She knew his game and she wasn't going to play it with him. After a few minutes charged with tension, she leaned forward and willed him to really hear her. "I see her every day when I drop off your sister. I've worked extremely hard this past week to procure a visitor pass for you. The one thing I will not tolerate from you is a lack of appreciation. If you can't sit here and talk to me with respect, then I will go on my way. That's it—I've put my cards on the table. Do you have a full house, or are you going to fold and listen to what I have to say?"

Kane narrowed his eyes. "What do you have to say that will make me respect you? How are you any different than all the others that make promises and in reality don't give a shit?" His shoulders relaxed a little.

Emily watched his body language. She picked up a twig that was near her and began to draw circles in the thin stream of water that was slowly moving along the curb. She wrote the word, 'mother.' In a soft voice, she said, "She really means a lot to you, doesn't she?"

Kane slowly nodded his head. A single tear slid down his cheek and he turned his face away. He was trying so hard to be unbreakable and strong, but his vulnerability was starting to show. "I love my mother. My mother and sister are the only ones left in my life who haven't abandoned me."

Emily put her hand on his shoulder and said, "I get that. And you and your sister are all she has left. She loves you so much and has missed you terribly. We talk about how to fix everything all of the time."

He looked at her again. This time he seemed to relax a little as he folded his hands in his lap.

Emily asked, "First things first. Do you need anything from the house? Backpack? Anything?"

He shook his head. "There's nothing in there but some of my clothes."

Emily stood up. "Okay...let's head to the hospital."

He stood immediately.

Emily put up her hand with her palm facing him. "I want a promise you will be on your best behavior. No foul language, no anger, just a nice day with your mother who is desperately trying to get better...." She put her hand down and asked, *"Comprendes?"*

Kane nodded.

Twenty minutes later, Emily was ready to open the hospital door. Karyn and Penny had no idea that Kane was coming to visit. Emily had stopped at a burger joint and picked up lunch for all of them. She could see that Kane was very nervous. He kept clasping his hands together and squeezing them. Although silent in the car, Emily could tell he was also excited.

Standing outside of the hospital door, Emily touched Kane on the shoulder and said, "Best behavior, right?" Then she pushed the door open.

When he walked through the door, two sets of eyes watched him enter. With screams of joy, the threesome was finally reunited. Emily watched as Kane hurried over to the bed and gave his mother a long and earnest hug. Tears of joy were running down both of their cheeks. Penny was jumping up and down and shrieks of excitement were coming from her lips. When things finally calmed down, Emily walked into the room. This time three sets of happy eyes looked at her.

Emily walked over to the bed and Karyn raised her hand to her. Emily graciously took her hand, squeezed it, and smiled. "I don't make idle promises, Karyn. I'm not your typical anything, so please trust me when I say you're all very special to me and I want to get you guys back together." She looked at Kane and winked. "I'm your supervisor today. I'm going to talk to the nurses and the doctor and I will be back in a while. Kane and I brought lunch for all of you, something a little tastier than hospital food." She handed Kane the large bag. "You cannot leave this room or I'm in trouble. I'm trusting you, Kane."

Karyn offered, her voice soft, "Thank you, Emily. We will be fine...won't we, Penny, Kane? We will abide by all of the rules, I promise."

Both children nodded.

Emily wanted to gain Kane's trust and to show him that not everyone was against him.

Once Emily left the room, the small celebration continued. Finally Karyn took Kane's hand and said, "I think Emily is different, Kane. I think she really does want to make things better for us. She's been helping me fill out papers for the state to get me some help with extra income, healthcare coverage, and maybe even a nicer home. She wants to set up counseling for us so we can get through the rough times. I'm asking you for your help."

Kane just nodded. His face showed his guarded cynicism.

The past two weeks were a lot easier than Emily had hoped for. With new cases every day, she was still working very hard towards getting Karyn's family settled. On a *pro-gratis* basis, one of her dear friends was taking Kane as a client and helping him. And as soon as Karyn was out of the hospital, she would start meeting with a family crisis therapist. Healthcare for Karyn and Penny and Kane came through, and it was very gratifying to Emily that Karyn wouldn't have to worry about her medical bills anymore.

Emily had also found a subsidy program that would sanction Karyn a section-eight housing voucher, allowing them to move into a three-bedroom apartment. Emily also knew that there would probably be a large settlement by the Metrorail for Karyn's injuries, but she didn't say anything. Kane had been on his best behavior, to everyone's surprise. He still had bouts of depression, but nothing that would spiral into violent episodes. He was beginning to learn how to control and overpower those ugly feelings that had once ruled his life.

Karyn could not be more appreciative for all the help. Emily had been her angel that she had spent the past years praying for, and it had only taken a 'near-death' accident to find her.

After six weeks in the hospital, the doctors were talking about releasing Karyn, providing her MS didn't react to the new medications and she continued to gain strength.

Two days before Karyn's release, Emily waltzed through the door, Penny in tow, with a big smile on her face. Penny was dancing around with excitement. None of her energy could be contained and she burst out into laughter. "We have a big surprise!" she blurted out.

Emily shook her head and said, "I knew you couldn't hold a secret very long. I should have bet you. At least I would have won some money!"

Karyn was getting out of bed and slipping into her robe. What is all this excitement about? What is the secret?"

"Emily will tell you, Mom."

Karyn laughed. "She will...?"

Emily gave Karen a hug. "I received some good news this morning at the office and that is why we are running late. I've applied for some housing for you. This morning I got two confirmations. One for you and the other for another wonderful and caring mother who needed help. Looks like two apartments opened up in a really nice housing complex and you were both the lucky recipients!"

"Mommy, I saw our new home and it's beautiful. There are so many kids my age and it even has a recreation room where I can go and hang out."

Karyn sat down on the bed and took a deep breath, speechless. She finally asked, "Where is it located and how far from work will I be?"

Emily avoided her question. She hopped onto the bed and sat down next to Karyn. Penny was already absorbed in a show that was on the television. "I'm so sorry, Karyn. I know all these changes are overwhelming and coming at you like speeding bullets. But since I was assigned to your case and you had been asking for help for years, without any response, I was not going to let that happen to you again." She took Karyn's hand. "I think we got everything into place. I'm just so happy. It killed me knowing how hard you worked and how you just couldn't catch up. It made me angry that your slumlord never fixed anything and I'm pushing to get that place condemned. I couldn't believe you only had hot water in the shower and not the bathtub. That tub was so cracked and pathetic. The sub-floor was caving in; and the kitchen sink that leaked was rotting your sub-floor, as well. The broken windows covered with plastic and the little heat was deplorable. You and your kids deserve better. So...now you have a new place in a fairly new complex subsidized by HUD."

Karyn didn't say anything. A single tear slid down her cheek. She squeezed Emily's hand. She was so choked up, speaking was a struggle. "Thank you."

Emily smiled. "I can't wait to get you moved in."

From across the room, Penny yelled, "I can't wait to move in. Mom, I love it!"

Karyn looked at her daughter who had already gone back to watching her favorite show. "What about Kane?" Karyn whispered.

Emily patted her hand and said, "I'm working on it. As soon as we get you situated, and if he continues to show progress, I'm going to fight for his release to you! My girlfriend said he is finally starting to open up to her and that is a good thing. He's been playing that 'blame game' for years now, using his father as his excuse to push everyone to their limit. He knew what he was doing and he didn't care. Getting into trouble was just masking his anger. Now, he's learning from his mistakes. Just wait and see!"

Karyn squeezed her hand. "When do I get to go home and pack?"

"You don't have to. The insurance company from Metrorail is paying for a company to come in and pack you up and out, then move you in. They are going to pay the rent for the next year while you recover. You will be on disability and receive a check every month, plus food stamps. Your boss has disability insurance, so you will receive a check there too."

"But I don't want handouts. I want to pay my own way. I'm not a moocher!"

"Moocher? W...h...a...t?" Emily's eyes opened wide, and she stared at Karyn in disbelief.

Karyn shook her head.

Emily's voice rose an octave. "You've just been in a major accident and in the hospital for over six weeks. YOU nearly DIED! Your MS flared up because of the accident, and I know you need some more recovery time. Aww hell, you could barely get out of bed today. You don't think I saw you struggle?" Emily sighed. "The only reason the doctors are going to release you is because I've begged my ass off and said you'd be better off at home with your children. I had to promise that the state would send a home health aide every day for at least four hours to help you clean, run errands, shop for groceries, and cook."

Karyn turned her head away as the tears began to flow.

"We know you are a hard worker. You need this time to heal." Emily slowly turned Karyn's head back toward her. "You deserve more time...don't you think?"

This time Karyn gradually nodded her head and then whispered, 'Why are you doing this for me and my family? I've waited for an angel for years to just give us a small break. No one ever listened or cared."

Emily swallowed the lump in her throat. "Life isn't fair sometimes. When they assigned me to you, I really didn't know what I would find or what degree of help you needed." She felt her emotions of the past week begin to peak. "Some people whine and cry about what they don't have and others silently deal and try to make it work. You, my dear sweet lady, have dealt with plenty."

Emily wiped away a wayward tear and asked with a smile, "Then we are finally on the same page?"


Emily knocked on the door and waited for someone to answer. She was tapping her toe as she nervously waited for it to open. She could barely hear Karyn yell through the closed door. "Hold on, I will be there in just a second!"

The door swung open and Karyn was sitting in her wheelchair. She had slowly rolled across the new wood floors. When she saw Emily standing at the door, a big smile crossed her face and she tried to straighten up, pulling the belt of her bathrobe a little tighter. She immediately tried to smooth down her short hair. "Sorry, I must look a mess. I was trying to clean up a little before Penny came home from school. We have been working really hard at settling in. I love my new place and Penny is over the moon." Karyn rolled her eyes. "She's met some wonderful girls in this complex that go to her school. I rarely see her anymore."

Emily just stood there. She hadn't moved an inch and had not said a word.

Karyn realized she had been blocking the entry with the wheelchair. "Oops. Here, let me move back." With weak arms, she managed to push the chair back to leave a passageway for Emily.

Emily still did not move. Instead, she said, "I'm so glad you are enjoying your new place."

Karyn laughed. "More than you will ever know!" She waved her hand. "Come on in."

"Okay, first you have to close your eyes. I have a surprise."

"Oh, for cripe's sake! Haven't you given us enough with all the wonderful used furniture and stuff you found us on Craigslist? That website is amazing. You can find everything you need for a home, cheap! Honestly...I feel like we stole Penny's bedroom set."

"I just love that darling bedroom set. Geez...every girl deserves a white trundle bed with a princess dresser to go with her pink walls. That was a great find!"

You're making this really hard for me to repay you for everything. It has got to stop!"

"Close those eyes! I swear you won't want to miss this surprise!"

"Only if you promise this is the last surprise ever! Go take all that energy and pass it to another family who needs it more."

"I think you're right! And I do have an appointment to meet with my new family this afternoon. They seem to be in a desperate state of chaos." She cleared her throat. "Close your eyes really tight!"

Karyn closed her eyes.

"Count slowly to ten and then open them. Oh, and don't scream or the neighbors might come running, or worse, call the paramedics. We don't need any big commotion."

"Nine...ten...." Karyn opened her eyes. She sucked in a deep breath and immediately stood up from her wheelchair. With open arms, she leaned forward and gave Kane the biggest hug she could ever remember giving him. He hugged her back and tears were sliding down his cheeks.

"I love you..." she whispered into his ear, loud enough for Emily could hear.

With his arms still wrapped around her, he whispered back, "I love you, too, Mom!"

Karyn glanced at Emily. "Thanks for letting him visit?"

Emily took the two suitcases from behind the wall, where they had been blocked from Karyn's view. "Nope, he's here to stay. He knows what he has to do. He's made some really strong promises, and they are giving him a second chance."

Karyn continued to hold on to her son.

Emily smiled at Kane and Karyn. "I'm so sorry about the train crash, but from the ashes rose a family. I'm just glad I got the opportunity to bring you back to a more stable place. I want all of you to keep me posted, and occasionally I will stop by for a visit."

"Anytime..." was all Karyn could push out.

"Hey, take Kane into his new room."

Kane looked at Emily and said, "I never had a bed to sleep in. Or a dresser for my clothes."

"Well, you do now. Enjoy your new home."

Karyn looked directly at Emily and said, "I don't know what more to say...."

"How about just 'goodbye.'"

Emily turned around and walked down the cement walkway. The sun was shining brightly, the sky was a perfect robin's egg blue, and there was barely a cloud to be seen. Emily inhaled a deep breath and exhaled it slowly. She was thinking about her new case and her meeting in an hour....

# CHAPTER 13

## Yun

The nurse came into the room and picked up the chart. She shook her head and said to herself, *"I don't know how this young child ever survived that crash? I hope she comes out of this coma and is okay. It's been weeks now...."* She checked all of the tubes and adjusted the position of the broken arm hanging in the air. She wiped the slight bit of saliva around Yun's mouth where one of the tubes laid and smoothed her wispy bangs off of her face. Walking around the bed, she picked up the chart and wrote all the stats down and then hung it back over the edge of the bed for the night nurses.

"Is there anything you need?" she asked the young man.

He shook his head, as he always did. He never said much. He had been there for a few days and rarely left the room. He slept on the small cot they brought in and only ate the food they brought him. His shy and quiet demeanor was really a cover for his inability to converse out of his own native language. He spoke little English and understood the sign language he and Katy had devised for the nurses. Katy didn't have a problem conversing with him, because of her fluency in Chinese. Thanks to Yun, who was now teetering near death, Chinese had almost become her second language and it was a good thing.

The young man stood up and walked toward the bed, like he had done a hundred times. The sound of all the machines that were keeping Yun alive was like a humming beehive. The bags filled with lifesaving fluids were methodically dripping into her body through all the tubes. Her heartbeat was being carefully monitored as the beeping sound filled the small, sterile room. Her heart had already flat-lined twice since she was brought to the hospital from the crash. At one point, the room filled up with doctors and nurses and they had almost not been able to revive her. One doctor refused to let her go. With every ounce of his strength, he was determined to keep her alive. After that horrendous day of non-stop casualties from the train crash, he was unwavering not to let another die. Especially not another young woman who was just starting out in life. He had already tried to save one, but he had needed a miracle and it didn't come through in time. So, while he feverishly pounded on Yun's chest and screamed out orders to the staff, miraculously, her heart began to beat again. Right after that moment, Dr. Ong sighed in pure relief, sat down, and privately said a few words of thanks for Yun Haun's young life.

The young man stood very quietly beside the bed. Very carefully, he took his painful and battered finger and touched the smooth skin on her face. Her small nose reflected their heritage and their dark hair was almost the same cropped length. Their features resembled each other, but nothing distinctive could ensure they were related. Her face was peaceful and the swelling and bruising was beginning to fade. Most of her injuries were internal, except for a nasty stitched gash that ran from her cheek to her ear. After being tossed around in the first car of the train, she had multiple broken bones and contusions, two punctured lungs, and had lost enough blood to nearly cost her—her life. If they would have gotten to her a few minutes later, she would have died. The triage knew exactly what to do, and with those few precious moments, they were able to sustain her life until they got her to the hospital. From there, and for the past few weeks, it was touch and go, with around the clock with nurses and doctors desperately trying to sustain her life. The crisis had peaked and now they were hopeful there would not be any lasting disabilities.

Chun laid his hand over hers as though he could give her his strength to survive. He didn't know what to say or do. He was not well versed in the culture of American women—or women at all. He had led a monkish life, taking care of his sick mother and helping to support his family. He slowly moved his finger over her beautiful Asian skin. He did not know her. He had never met her and his parents had rarely talked about her. He knew he had a sister, but that was basically all he was told. Just before his mother died, she had handed him a sealed envelope, begging him to open it only at the death of his father. So, with respect for her, he had tucked it away in his few personal items—never to bring it out, until the requested time.

He missed his mother and father. His mother was never completely healthy since the trip she had taken to another country. Nobody knew much and he valued his parents' privacy.

His father finally told him the story of Yun one evening, just before he passed away. He made Chun open up the envelope and then he read him the name—Yun Haun. Listed below was an address, along with another name—Sun Lee Yang. Not knowing what to do with the information and feeling awkward for invading their secret past, which had been hidden for so long, Chun tucked the envelope away under the grass mat in his room.

It wasn't until ten days earlier that his life took an all-encompassing change. Out of nowhere, on a rainy day, he noticed a letter placed under the front door of his hut. The dampness of the rain and humidity had caused some of the writing to become blurred, but he did recognize his name, Chun Haun. Chun was not well-educated in reading, so he walked to the nearby village ten miles away to have one of the elders read it to him. Inside the letter, it explained the need for him to come to the United States, due to an emergency. There was a visitor visa, along with enough cash to purchase a plane ticket and help him along the way. There was also a name to contact when he finally got to Los Angeles—Katy Blackwald.

The request asked that he travel as soon as possible, because of the medical necessity of his sister. A sister who was never spoken of and he knew nothing about—except that she lived in the United States. It had always been a dream of his and his family, that one day, he would travel to the states and make a better life for himself. But he had never been presented an opportunity and going under these circumstances made him feel sad. But this was his only chance.

So he took what little he had and booked his flight.


Chun walked off the plane with just a small backpack containing all of his worldly possessions. He was dressed in the best clothing he owned, and yet, it still barely met the standards that was socially suitable in this part of the world. With his eyes narrowed, his back rigid and his head held high, he walked through the tunnel leading to the main terminal. Immediately, he caught his breath at the size and activity that surrounded this large International airport located in the heart of Los Angeles. He had never been out of his small village in China, let alone crossed thousands and thousands of miles to a country he knew little about. Uncertainty crossed his face and he stood paralyzed and disorientated. Suddenly, a hand touched his shoulder and he spun around to see who it belonged to. Too scared to utter a word, he just stood and stared at the beautiful young girl in front of him.

The sweet smile on the young lady's face was enchanting and he couldn't stop staring at her long blonde hair that swayed around her shoulders as she started to speak. Knowing very little English, panic began to cross his face as he flushed with fear. How was he going to communicate?

Surprising him by switching to his own tongue, the young woman introduced herself.

"Nǐ hǎo, Chun, wǒ jiào, Katy." She held out her hand and waited for his response.

A sigh of relief and a slight smile began to replace the panic he had just felt. He held out his hand. She continued, "I'm your sister's roommate at college and her best friend." She spoke in a soft voice that showed off her flawless Chinese. "I'm sure the letter I sent you was a great surprise. If it wasn't for Yun's health, I would have wished this was done on a family visit, not an emergency. I want to personally thank you for coming. Yun and I deeply appreciate it." Tears began to well in her eyes, then she said, "I appreciate it, because your sister has had a tough time."

Chun nodded his head to acknowledge her kind words. "Is she still in the hospital?"

"Yes...."

"Will she be okay?" he asked.

"We're not sure. It depends on you."

"On me? What could you possibly need from me that I came all the way from home?"

"To see if you are a compatible match."

"Match? For what...?" he asked, looking confused.

"She sustained many severe injuries, one of which has caused complications with her kidneys. We didn't know what to do and we could not find her a match in the computerized donors."

"Computerized donors?" He looked puzzled, again.

Katy nodded her head. "Sun Lee Yang, her adopted mother, was very leery to release any information about the whereabouts of her birth family. It took a lot of coaxing for her to give me the name of the area and village that you live in. I found you sooner that I thought and I'm hopeful that you might be able to help."

"Help her how?" He looked confused. "I have nothing of any value. I'm afraid I won't be of much help."

"Time is not on our side and she has had a lot of setbacks with her recovery. The one we are most concerned with is that she is on continuous dialysis. Both her kidneys are failing."

Chun's eyes opened wide. His mother had died of kidney failure after a short illness. "I'd be happy to help any way I can. But, I'm not a rich man, nor do I have anything except what is in my pocket." He pulled out a small bundle of American dollars. "And this is what you sent me."

"We aren't looking for money...she might need a kidney and we were hoping you are a match. Would you be willing to donate one of your kidneys to keep her alive?" Katy could visually feel her heart beating out of her chest as she waited for his response.

Chun turned his head to look out a nearby window, and then he took a deep breath. He smiled at a small child playing with its mother. He turned back and said, "If my sister needs a kidney, then she shall have one of mine. She's the only 'blood' that runs the same as mine. Everyone is gone. My mother and father have passed to another life, and with no siblings in China, I have nothing to go back to right now."

A tear spilled over on her cheek as the relief of his answer hit her deep in her heart.

He reached over with a bruised finger and caught the tear.

Katy tried to grin. "We will have to have you tested."

He shook his head. "No reason to test me. I am her perfect match."

"But we don't know that. Sometimes brothers and sisters don't carry the same DNA."

He looked deeply into her eyes. "Twins carry the same DNA."

Katy gasped as she sucked in a large breath. "You are her twin, not her brother!?"

The serious look on his face let Katy know that he was not joking. "The story is that my mother was tested and found to be carrying twins. The doctors wanted to abort her pregnancy, but she would not allow them. Instead, she came here, had her twins, and took me home. She was only allowed one child by the government and she wanted both of her children to live."

Katy exhaled the breath she had been holding. "Oh my god! How awful that your mother had to make a choice between you both...."

"She kept us both alive. It took every yen she had saved to get to America to give birth. When she came home—she died with that burden of regret and a heart that had broken that day she gave birth. The regret that she never got to hold her baby girl or see her first smile haunted her."

Katy stood there looking down at the ground, in deep concentration.

Chun broke the silence. "My sister received the gift of life and a great country. I received my loving parents. The least I can do is keep her alive." He touched Katy's shoulder, and when she looked up, he said, "Life is never without struggle. No matter who you are or where you come from."

Katy looked at this gentle young man standing in front of her and took his hand and began to walk. Then she spoke in a soft voice, "Come on, I need to get you to the hospital. Yun has no idea that you are here.

Finding you was the only way she could survive."

He nodded his head and pursed his lips. "She will survive. She's a fighter."

"How do you know that?"

"She is my sister, and my family is from strong mules."

Katy laughed. "Well, I hope she's strong enough to forgive me for finding you without her permission."

The room was full. They were all trying to figure out why Yun had not surfaced from the doctor-induced coma. They had technically done everything they possibly could to gradually bring her out. Their only conclusion was that there was some kind of brain damage that was holding her in the induced state.

Yun's head was pounding in agony from all of the noise. The loud voices were creating an intense need for her to say something so she could continue to sleep. Finally, she barely opened her eyes as her lips whispered, "Please be quiet!"

Everyone's eyes rotated toward the bed as the silence in the room created the peace Yun was hoping for. With her eyes barely open, she looked around the room and noticed all the attention riveted on her. Everyone swiftly began to gather around the bed to see what she was going to say next. They stood there with their jaws dropped open as they continued to watch her. Her eyes slowly began to circle the bed to see the violators of her silence.

Unable to take the stillness, Katy said, "Even when she's barely slipping back into consciousness she has to say 'please.'" A shaky laugh escaped her and she clasped Yun's slight fingers between her own.

Dr. Ong stepped forward and bent down, took Yun's other hand, and looked into her eyes. His face lit up with a big smile. "Looks like we have this little princess back with us again."

The nurses could be heard clapping their hands and showing tremendous excitement. They had worked so hard to keep her alive and no one was sure what degree of damage her brain injuries had caused. Dr. Ong was worried about the increased pressure, bleeding, and loss of oxygen she had sustained in the first few days. He hoped that with the fast response of the triage, they had stopped any permanent harm. Many had their doubts, but those uncertainties were washed away with Yun's three simple words.

Katy sat quietly and watched her dear friend. Tears of joy were streaming down her face. She wanted to grab her shoulders and yell at the top of her lungs, "You scared me to death!" But the reality of it took a different turn. Instead, she kissed each of Yun's fingers. Yun smiled at her friend and shut her eyes again. She drifted back to her peaceful cocoon.

Hours later, the nurses were able to coach her into more specific demands to prove that she was emerging from her fragile state with her senses still intact.

"How many fingers am I holding up?" Dr. Ong asked.

"My eyes are blurred, I'm not sure," Yun whispered.

"What's your name?" He continued.

"Yun. Who are you?" she asked.

"Your doctor. And I'm so glad to finally get to meet you."

"What happened, why am I here? I don't remember anything other than a loud whistle and a lot of noise."

He smiled down at her. "There was a loud whistle, I'm told. Just before the train crashed into the truck that was stuck on the tracks. You've had a tough time of it. You've been in a coma for weeks. The only setback we are having is with your kidneys. They've closed down on us a few times and now they are barely functioning. I don't want you to worry about it right now. We've got it covered."

It was too much information for Yun to absorb, so she closed her eyes and went back to sleep. Quietly sitting in the corner of the room was her brother. He had been there for over a week, waiting with an extraordinary amount of patience. After Yun had closed her eyes, he got up from his seat and walked over to the bed. He looked at the doctor and asked in broken English, "I will do for her. When will be the operation?"

Dr. Ong looked at the young man and smiled. In perfect Chinese, he said, "I speak your tongue. My parents are from Beijing. I was there as a small boy and then my family moved to the States."

Chun smiled. Dr. Ong placed his hand on his shoulder and said, "That is so kind of you. The only thing that stops her recovery is the constant battle with dialysis. She needs it for a few more weeks until we get her strong enough to go through another big surgery. If we are lucky, she will be able to function normally. Are you sure you want to do this?"

"Yes, I'm sure."

A few days later, Chun was sleeping on the cot in the back corner of the room. Suddenly, he heard horrifying screams indicating something was terribly wrong. Yun's shrieking was loud and incessant. Not sure what was going on, Chun rushed over to her side and gripped the guardrail. Her eyes were closed and her face contorted. With a jolt, she opened her eyes and looked directly at him, abruptly stopping her shrieking. At that moment, a nurse came bursting through the door and shoved Chun to the side while she checked on Yun. With a sigh of relief, the nurse realized it wasn't a medical problem and just a nightmare. Turning to Chun with a reddened face, she apologized profusely for her rough behavior and exited the room. Chun stood at the end of the bed and stared at Yun.

In return, she stared at him and then whispered, "I'm sorry. I must have had a nightmare. You must have other patients to look after. Thank you for all your concern."

Chun replied, "I'm not with the hospital. I am here for you."

His Chinese was impeccable. "Me? I don't recognize you..." she questioned in his language of choice.

He arched his short and narrow eyebrows. "That is because we never met. I came here from China when they asked me to. They said you were in grave condition and I would be able to help." His face did not show any confliction of his broad statement.

"Help me?" She looked very confused. "How could you possibly help me? And who asked you to?"

In a low voice, barely audible, Chun answered, "Kate."

Yun tried to sit up. The conversation was getting really confusing and her restlessness was beginning to show. "What? Why?"

Without a single flinch or a show of shyness, he bluntly said, "I am Chun, your twin brother. They said you needed a kidney."

Yun's eyes opened as wide as they could and her face showed considerable shock at the statement this young man just made. She threw her head back into the pillow and closed her eyes as she tried to absorb his words. Her heart was beating out of her chest and her breaths were coming quick and short. What she really wanted to do was inhale a deep pocket of air and scream, but that didn't happen. Instead, her hands grabbed the sheets and she held on tight.

Chun noticed her anxiety. "I know this might come as a shock, but please don't let it get you so upset." He bent over the bed and touched her hand that was turning white as it clinched the sheets. "I will explain everything."

She did not move and would not open her eyes. This was worse than the nightmare she had just experienced. She wasn't sure now if she had woke up or if this was just a continuation of that frightening dream. She just wanted to go back to sleep and be left alone.

"Please open your eyes. I'm sorry if I scared you. My intentions were to let you know who I am and why I am here. It was not meant to create more problems for your recovery."

She laid there perfectly still and all he could see was that her heart continued to beat at an enormous speed.

Chun let go of her hand and began to turn away. "I will catch a plane today...." He looked confused and dejected.

Suddenly Yun opened her eyes and pleaded, "Don't go."

Chun turned back and a small sigh escaped his lips. "Let me get a chair and move it close to the bed and I will tell you the whole story as I learned it from our parents."

Tears welled in her eyes when she heard him say, 'our parents.' They weren't her parents. She knew nothing about them. She never got to look into her mother's face to acknowledge her as the woman who gave her life. She never spoke her name, because it was never given to her. And when her brother said, "Her name was Yuni," an unfathomable pain hit deep in her heart. An ache that was not from her injuries, but from a lifetime of agony she felt for a mother who never got to pick up her daughter.

Yun looked at her brother as the tears began to stream down her face. "I would like to hear it all, as I know nothing of my past. I feel like I have lost a lifetime."

Chun understood what she was saying, but it was hard for him to relate. He had his parents for all those years and in spite of being poor and from root beginnings, he had parental love and joy.

That night a lifetime of shadows abated and two strangers began to get to know each other. Yun had dreamed of a time she would get to meet her family. But the years had not been kind to her mother and father, and only her brother was left to continue the Haun dynasty. They talked of their childhoods. Chun sat for hours telling her stories to familiarize her with the parents she would never get to meet. He wanted her to know how beautiful her mother was and how strong their father was. Yun closed her eyes and listened until she drifted off to sleep.

It was a night that was a long time coming. One that finally let Yun sleep in peace.


Yun was laying on the gurney in her room, waiting for Katy to arrive. She was scared of her future and what was to come. Everything was changing so rapidly. Dealing with her injuries and her kidneys had slowed down her recovery and triggered so many emotional uncertainties, for weeks, as she listened to the doctors and tried hard to get strong enough for the surgery.

Yun was thinking how thankful she was that Chun had unselfishly offered her a better life, free of dialysis. As he explained to her one evening, "I came to help in any way I could. I knew it was the right thing and I knew our mother's wish would be the same. We are family—you are my sister."

Weeks of getting to know her brother had finally brought Yun a calm forgiveness for her parents. For years she wavered between hatred and rejection, always wondering why they had left her all alone to survive on her own with a family who didn't love her enough.

Katy ran into the room, out of breath. She looked at her dear friend and touched her shoulder. "I found it!" She handed the thin gold chain with a gold coin on it to Yun. "Damn...with all the chaos the day of the crash, this was the only thing that I had to identify you. When they handed me this necklace, I knew I had to put it somewhere safe. Then I forgot where I put it. For the past hour I've been tearing the apartment apart looking for it. And, you know, silly me...I finally put something where it really belonged...hanging on your dresser mirror!" Katy sighed with exasperation.

Yun grinned at her friend, who was showing her nervous jitters. "Thank you. I wanted to bring the necklace with me into the operating room. I don't care if I wear it or it sits under my pillow. It's been my good luck charm for years."

Katy's eyes opened wide and she gave Yun a look of disbelief. "How can you say that? You were wearing it when the train crashed. That was NOT lucky!" She handed the necklace to Yun.

Yun smiled. "Yes, it was! I could have died and I didn't."

Katy shook her head at Yun's last remark. "Oh man...you just crack me up! Okay, you were *lucky....*" She dramatically rolled her eyes.

Yun smiled at her crazy, dear friend.

Dr. Ong stepped into the room at that moment and walked over to the gurney. He asked, "Are you ready?"

Yun grinned. "Not really. I'm terrified. Not for me, but for Chun."

Dr. Ong gave her a questioning look.

"He doesn't have to do this. I can wait for a registered donor. This means he will only have one kidney left."

"He wants to do it, Yun. He wants you to have a normal life again. He's a strong young man and he should be fine. Many family members give up kidneys for their relatives." He bent down and whispered loudly, "Besides, this might mean he can petition for permanent residency...with my help."

Yun smiled. "I would love him to stay and get an education. You would do that? You would help us?"

"Yes, so look at the positive...."

The door opened and they wheeled Chun in on his gurney and put it next to Yun's. His eyes were closed and he looked very relaxed. When he heard the voices, he turned his head.

Dr. Ong asked, "How are you feeling, Chun? Are you sure you want to do this?"

Chun nodded. "She is my other half. There is no answer other than yes."

Yun reached out her hand. "Thank you."

Chun reached across and grasped her hand and brought it toward his chest.

Suddenly, the necklace feel out of her hand and landed on Chun's bed. He released her hand and picked it up to look at it. His eyes opened wide with surprise as he twisted and turned the shiny gold necklace. Then he closed his eyes and laid his hand on his chest, still grasping the chain. He inhaled and released two deep breaths. Everyone watched this unusual reaction from Chun. He was never a very emotional or expressive young man. Simple and forward was how he reacted to life.

Yun whispered, "Chun, are you having second thoughts? You don't have to do this. I'll be fine. We'll find someone else."

He opened his eyes and looked directly at Yun. In a very low voice, he said, "Where did you get this necklace?"

Yun shrugged her shoulders. She could not understand why he was questioning her about the necklace. "It was given to me when I was very young by my adopted mother. She never said anything. She just handed it to me one day without an explanation. It was the first piece of jewelry I ever received from anyone. So, I have cherished it my entire life. I call it my good luck charm. It's just a simple necklace."

He pulled his gown down in the front and hanging around his neck was a similar half coin on a beautiful gold chain. "Our mother put this around my neck as a very young boy. I often wondered who had the other half or what she did with it. I never asked and she never said anything. But I wore it proudly because she put it around my neck."

Yun was stunned.

Chun held her necklace next to his and the two half coins fit perfectly together. Then he reached out his hand and dropped her necklace into her outstretched hand. He looked up at the ceiling and whispered, "Maybe you were meant to be in that train crash. Maybe that moment of impact was meant to bring our lives together? Maybe it was our mother's divine intervention?"

"Maybe..." Yun said, her voice shaking with emotion.

Dr. Ong broke the silence. "The surgeons are scrubbed and ready to start. Are you both ready?"

Both heads nodded as they laid back on their pillows.

Dr. Ong looked at each sibling and then he looked directly at Yun. "In ten hours, you are going to be carrying the kidney of your brother. This could be your start to a new journey in life. It was just a miracle Katy found him in the middle of China, working in a small village."

"All I ever wanted in life was to meet my family. I knew I had a brother, but it was a total shock to find he was my twin." She smiled at Chun. "I feel so honored to have him here and for this lifesaving gift he's giving me."

Chun turned to his sister with a very humbled expression on his face.

Katy was standing off to the side. She had watched the whole exchange and knew exactly where this new journey would take them. It was the beginning of a new family that had been away from each other for far too long. The moment of impact had changed their lives forever....

# CHAPTER 14

## Terrence

Terrence had laid in the wreckage, only half conscious. The other half was 'walking on the edge' and on the verge of passing out. He knew the train had crashed, because he felt the impact and, unexpectedly, his muscled body was thrown through the air like a weightless astronaut. Only, within seconds, flying metal seats and other objects came toward him like hurtling projectiles. Out of the corners of his eyes, he also watched as other travelers were being thrown around. It had been terrifying when the large passenger car heaved into the air and came down, rolling over a few times, crushing the metal all around him.

When the passenger car had finally come to a complete stop, Terrence's life flashed before his eyes. His eyes were closed and he could not move. It felt like a heavy weight was pinning him down and a crushing pain was searing through his right leg. He thought it odd that he could not feel his left leg. He moved both arms, which seemed to be unrestricted but badly injured and bleeding. He was shaken to the very core of his being and he didn't know what to do as panic began to set in. His life had come to a standstill— just like the once bouncing train.

There were loud, hysterical screams, people crying out in fear, and finally police sirens and ambulances. He turned his head just slightly to his left and he saw the pretty young lady who boarded the train just before him. Her body was crushed by the weight of metal wreckage. He wanted to help her, but he could not move. His legs were pinned down and he was helpless to do anything but lay there and wait for aid. It was at that moment, that he finally realized how very lucky he was to still be alive.

A large piece of metal was pinning down the lower half of his body. The tremendous pain was more than he could handle. Sweat broke out from his brow as he too began to yell for help, hoping someone, anyone, could hear him. He slowly moved his hand to his right leg. He felt his torn flesh and a lot of blood. He went to touch his left leg, but he couldn't feel a thing, nor could he find it. Fear of the unknown, the horrific pain, the visions all around him were more than he could handle. He closed his eyes and passed out....

It took the firemen and emergency staff twenty precious minutes to extract him from the twisted metal that barely resembled a train car anymore. After evaluating his condition within seconds, an EMT placed a tight tourniquet around the top of his left leg to keep him from bleeding out. The right leg was crushed and bones were protruding from his torn flesh. The crew instantly knew that getting him out of there was a matter of life or death. He had lost a lot of blood and they were just praying there was no life-threatening internal damage. They desperately needed to get him to the hospital in time to give him transfusions and emergency attention. Every second was costly as blood pumped out of his open wounds.

While six EMTs worked on him and gave him a few units of blood, they pumped him full of pain medications to ease the tremendous agony he was enduring. Wavering between consciousness and delirium, his screams of pain were sending shock waves through everyone who could hear. When they finally extracted him from the twisted metal, a surgery room had been prepared for his arrival. One leg needed to be amputated and the other was only hanging on by a few muscles and tendons.

Terrence's mother and son were contacted by the hospital once his identification was validated. They rushed to the hospital with little information to prepare them. Two doctors took them into a private room and the chief of surgery reluctantly let them know that Terrence had lost one leg and they were trying to save the other. He explained all of the details of what Terrence had already gone through in a short time. He explained the further procedures they needed to perform to save his other leg. The news was devastating and almost seemed surreal to Vera Martin. After all, her son had rarely suffered any sick days in his life and he was such a productive and physically active young man. And now, he was lying in bed with doctors struggling to save his life, a life with every probability of being spent in a wheelchair.

*"How did this happen?"* Vera asked herself over and over. *"Will he survive the loss or will he fall apart?"*

Unprepared for the worst, Vera Martin and her grandson where thrown into a world of confusion and anxiety. Finally, feeling overwhelmed and on the verge of losing it, they were privately ushered into a special waiting room that was limited to immediate families of the critical train victims. Doctors and nurses were constantly walking in and out of the waiting room, communicating with the families.

The thought of Vera's only child dying was almost more than she could handle. As she sat down on the couch, she brought out her rosary beads and began to pray. Timothy took charge and acknowledged the updates of Terrence's condition with a 'moving forward' type of approach. He bombarded the doctors with questions and was relentless in his communications with all of the staff in the ICU.

For the next few days, all they could do was hope that Terrence would make it through and that his only leg could be reattached and saved. They waited in the hospital for days as Terrence went through one surgery after another. The orthopedic doctors conversed daily with Timothy and his grandmother. After a week had passed, they felt comfortable that Terrence was out of trouble and that his survival would now depended on his emotional state of mind.

Under heavy debilitating pain medications, his state of mind did not show much clarity and his awareness was limited. He knew his mother and son were there for support, but that was his limit. His son had to constantly remind him that he was in the hospital and that it was a train crash he had been in. Slowly, over the next week as his haziness began to clear, he began to get stronger and ask more questions. When he found out he had lost one leg, there was no consoling him. After all, his whole life had revolved around his ability to play professional sports. It was his career and his love of the game that had kept him there. Thinking about spending the rest of his life in a wheelchair created a depression that no one could break through. Not his mother, not his son, not the owners of his team or his teammates who showed up, faithfully, with words of encouragement.

The psychological trauma overwhelmed his ability to cope and left him feeling suicidal, repulsed with his physical mutilation. He had lost control over his life. Emotional bouts of depression were something he was not used to. He felt trapped in a body that was no longer useful and a helplessness to not be able to do anything about it. He was filled with shame. Seeing his son every day, knowing what a failure he had become, was more than Terrence could handle. That inflamed male ego he once carried became an albatross around his neck.

The meeting he was going to the on fateful day of the crash was exactly what his business manager expected. When Terrence didn't show up, his manager went into the meeting alone. His contract was pulled, and with only one year left, they decided to cut him from the team. They had opened him up as a free agent, but that wasn't going anywhere. No teams had stated any interest because his potential and stats were not meeting the criteria any of the teams were looking for. He was too old, too damaged, and too expensive to maintain—even with two healthy legs. So with mutual respect, the team decided to pay off his remaining year and cut him. They had not even offered him the minor leagues this time. Their philosophy was that the younger players coming up were cheap and talented. Terrence was old, worn out, and had given nearly ten years of his life making great money and endearing adulation from the fans. Ten years for a professional player was a great run. Most players barely made it to the majors; and if you were lucky enough, a few good years was considered a decent career and long enough to have your own trading card. Only a chosen few made it in the major leagues for more than twenty years. That was unheard of unless you were Cal Ripken, Jr., Nolan Ryan, Tommy John, or Alex Rodriquez.

Terrence knew they were going to cut him. He had that feeling when he boarded the train that morning. He just never could imagine the day would end with losing a leg and a near death experience. Nor, did he want his career to end this way. His life had been too good and too happy. He had enjoyed his job and all the perks that went with it. Now, everything was at an end and the probability of him being offered any kind of a coaching job was nonexistent. His life was like the twisted metal they had pulled him from; it had spun one hundred and eighty degrees.

As he laid there beating himself up emotionally, the thought of suicide began to fill his mind. They were temporarily laid to rest as Terrence thought about Timothy.

His son had a smile that lit up the room. But the positive attitude that Timothy brought with him every day when he visited was almost more than Terrence could bear.

Terrence was a hands-on father and he had always been there for Timothy. He taught Timothy how to be a man and deal with any given situation. He had pumped him up when he studied all night and still failed the test. He refused to let Timothy be a quitter and had lovingly pushed him to be the best he could.

Now Terrence was lying in bed a broken old man, wallowing in self-pity, and thinking of ways he could check-out of life. Terrence was letting the crash take everything he had and throw it to the curb. He had ultimately become a bitter victim of a moment of impact that was beyond his control.

The door opened and Timothy bounced into the room and stood next to the bed. "Hey, Pops, what's going on? How was your day?"

Terrence turned his head away and grunted.

"The doctor told me that your stump is healing and they think you may be able to use a prosthetic soon." Timothy looked happy and his smile went from cheek to cheek.

Terrence growled, "I hate when you call my leg a stump."

Timothy went around to the other side of the bed to look at his dad's face. "Are we going to have another one of those days where you have a pity party and only invite yourself? Nana won't even come anymore, because you have gotten so mean and angry."

Terrence's eyes narrowed. "So what if I am?"

Timothy moved closer and picked up his dad's hand. "I'm not going to let you. You were once a great ball player and now you can be a great something else! Lots of people evolve, because they have no other choice. Didn't you always tell me that when I failed my spelling tests?" He bent over his dad. "Didn't you tell me I wasn't great at spelling, but I was amazing with math and science? You wouldn't let me cry about a little spelling test."

Terrence's voice began to crack and become gruff. "A spelling test and losing your leg and career are two very different things." He pointed to the door. "Why don't you leave me alone? I'm tired and I need some space."

Timothy backed away from the bed and narrowed his eyes. His smile had disappeared and his anger was beginning to surface. "Your career was already over, Dad. It's time to move on. How long are you going to keep pulling this 'leave me alone' shit?" His voice raised higher. "Do you really want me and Nana to leave you alone? If that's what you want, then I won't come back. You fucking piss me off, Dad!"

Terrence raised himself off his pillow slightly. "Don't you use that trash mouth around here. I thought I taught you better than that!"

Timothy stomped to the door and grasped the handle tightly. "You taught me not to be a coward and all I see is this scared old man lying in bed crying over one lousy leg. Some example you're setting now." Timothy's hands started shaking. "We could have buried you! Fuck you!" Timothy yanked open the door and ran out into the hallway. Timothy had never talked to his father with disrespect before, but he was getting tired of his negative attitude.

Timothy ran out the door and right into Dr. Ong. Tears were streaming down his face. Dr. Ong put his arms around Timothy's small body and hugged him close to his chest. "I know your dad is giving you a hard time. He's giving everyone a hard time. Right now he's like a keg of gun powder ready to explode."

Timothy looked up. "My Nana won't come to visit anymore. She said he is not the son she raised. He's been really mean to her." Timothy inhaled a deep breath. "I want him to stop being mean."

Dr. Ong moved slightly away, and said, "Come with me to my office. Let's talk about this. I bet you and I can come up with some way to snap him out of his bitterness. "

Timothy followed as the tears continued to travel down his cheeks.

Vera was doing what she did every day. She was placing a plate filled with eggs, bacon, and potatoes on the table for Timothy. She turned and walked over to the refrigerator to get him a glass of milk. "I don't know, Timothy. I think your father might get mad and then it might throw him into a deeper depression. I've stayed away because he seems to blame me...for what...I don't know. I thought maybe he needed some space."

Timothy was frowning. "It's not you, Nana. He blames everyone. What he doesn't see is all the people who died and the ones that are still in the hospital with horrible injuries compared to his. I know he's lost a leg, and another that is barely going to hold him up, but he should be happy he is still alive. I know someone spared his life...."

Vera sat down at the table and pushed the glass of milk toward Timothy. She was on the verge of crying. "I'm glad he's still here.

Terrence doesn't know how lucky he is. But...he has to learn that on his own."

Timothy stood up and started to move around the room. "Don't you see, Nana? This is why I have to do...what I have to do. Otherwise, he'll continue to be angry the rest of his life."

"Timothy...."

"Nana, people lose legs and arms and all kinds of things all the time. People get cancer and die. My friend Joey lost his mother a few weeks ago when a drunk driver killed her as she was walking across the street. Another boy lost his father to war. Dad needs to appreciate that he's still alive." Timothy drank his whole glass of milk in one long gulp. "Dr. Ong showed me so many people in worse shape than my pops and I'm going to let him know."

Vera sighed and ruffled the hair on her grandson's head. She had been the closest thing to a mother Timothy had ever had in his life. Eleven years ago, Vera had seen Terrence display the same anger and depression when Timothy was placed in his arms and Sophie walked away from all her responsibilities. Terrence held onto the resentment and rage that crippled him for the first year. But, on Timothy's first birthday, when he didn't receive a card or a gift, Terrence knew what he had to do. With the strength of a lion, he moved forward and never looked back, nor did he ever trust a woman again. Not once did he have any serious relationships, or ever introduce his son to his quick flings that never lasted long enough to develop into a relationship. He focused on being the best father possible.

Vera stood up and walked toward the wall next to the back door. She reached up and took her sweater from the hook. "If you think this might work, then let's go see."

Timothy crammed the last strip of bacon into his mouth. He chewed it quickly and then said, "I don't know if it will work. But I can't just let my dad lay in bed hating life and wishing he were dead. He needs a dose of reality and Dr. Ong and I think this is the best way we can show him that his life has not ended—it's just beginning again."

Vera wondered how he had gotten so smart and what made him become the man of the house. His values and his love were a reflection from the only two people in his life. With no other relatives, their small family had persevered. "What if he doesn't want to go? What will you do then?"

Timothy turned his head to look directly at his grandmother. "There is no 'if' in my vocabulary right now. My dad needs to find a light before the darkness destroys him. It's like Darth Vader and his son."

Vera ruffled her grandson's hair and smiled. "Darth who? Do I know your friend?"

Timothy began to laugh. "No, Nana...I will tell you that story later today. Right now, we need to get to the hospital."

Vera sighed. "You young kids know everything nowadays. Technology has fed your brains with so much information. Okay, let's see what we can do."

They both walked out of the door. They were on a mission and nothing was going to stop Timothy from helping his father.

Later, at the hospital, Timothy walked through his dad's door, pushing his grandmother in a wheelchair and doing wheelies. When the chair almost fell over, they burst into laughter.

Terrence watched their antics with narrowed and wary eyes. "What the hell are you doing? You could hurt your grandmother roughhousing like that!"

Ignoring his dad, Timothy popped another wheelie.

"I said stop that!" Terrence yelled.

"Make me! You've been too angry that Nana and I wanted to have some fun. Can I get you to take a walk with us? I'll even push, and I promise not to pop a wheelie!" Timothy challenged him.

Terrence closed his eyes and blocked everyone out. He had been doing that for a few weeks. His choice to not answer his son's question threw Timothy into a rage.

Timothy hissed through his teeth with an anger that far surpassed his father's, "You have no clue what life is about. You never did. All you did was prance your ass around on a baseball field while stroking your ego," Timothy took another big breath and began at the top of his lungs, "so you lost a leg. Big deal! Do you know how many people in this world have lost legs? So many more have lost a lot more than that. They've lost their children, their parents, and dear friends.... You can replace a leg...but can you replace me?"

Nana stood in the corner and watched as a young boy turned the tables on his father and gave him one of life's hardest lessons.

"All you've done is wallow in your self-pity and think about yourself. Well, open your eyes! You have two people in this room who love you very much! We're sorry this happened and it's just as painful to us as to you, especially watching you slowly die inside. You are alive...so quit acting like you're dead." Timothy's voice softened. "Show me the stuff you are really made of. Show me how you don't give up on life and that you keep moving forward no matter how hard the times get. Show me that I'm worth living for and that I can look up to you as a son should look up to his father. Show me that young boy Nana said you were and how you barreled through your entire life with an intensity that got you into the big leagues." Timothy walked slowly to the bed and sat on the edge next to his father. He wrapped two loving arms around his dad's shaking shoulders, laid his head on his dad's strong chest, and began to cry. It was the first real cry he had since seeing his father the first week. His sobs could be heard through the room, piercing the hearts of all who could hear them.

Terrence wrapped his arms around his son and held him tight. Timothy's shaking body was more than he could handle. In a low whisper, he said, "I guess my arms were saved so that I could still hold you close. At least I have that." Terrence began to weep.

Quietly, Vera walked out of the room. The scene had almost been more than she could emotionally handle. She knew that father and son had to reestablish their broken relationship and she didn't want to intrude on something so private. Vera went into the visitor lounge and waited. An hour later, the door to the room opened and Timothy came out, pushing the wheelchair. Sitting in the wheelchair was his father. Timothy wheeled the chair toward Vera and stopped in front of her.

"Dad and I are going down to the fourth floor. Would you like to come?"

Vera smiled. "Sure. What's on the fourth floor?"

"The rehab for Pops. He promised he would try to be the fastest guy on the team again."

Vera grinned and nodded. "Let's go."

225

When the elevator doors opened, the enormous glass windows displayed lots of patients working with doctors and nurses and in all stages of physical activity. The fourth floor reminded Timothy of a large gymnasium where everyone was doing their own thing—only this room had a circus-like atmosphere. Everyone was lifting, standing, walking, pushing, and juggling balls, trying to overcome their disabilities. Prosthetic legs and arms were noticeable, but not necessarily a handicap as they worked with their private trainers. Three men were off in a corner playing basketball in their wheelchairs.

A young girl was trying out a new set of legs, while a soldier, who was wearing his army hat, tried to catch a ball with two prosthetic arms. It was encouraging to Timothy and Vera, but Terrence's face showed his discomfort.

Timothy pushed him further into the room. He bent down next to his father and said, "This is really cool, Dad. Dr. Ong said we would find this a fun place with a whole lot of nice people. What do you think, Dad?" His head swung around in all directions, taking everything in.

Terrence looked at his son's excited face. "I think this is where all the broken toys go. Doctors try to fix them, but they will never be the same. Just like me...I will never be able to run with you again. I might not even walk." He sighed and looked down at his lap.

"That's not so, Dad. You just got a second chance at life while you're still young enough to find something else to excel at."

"Like what?"

"I don't know. Look at Bethany Hamilton, who lost her arm during a shark attack. She's ranked one of the best surfers around and is on all the magazine covers." He smiled. "You of all baseball players should look at Jim Abbott, the pitcher for the Angels. He was a first round draft pick in 1988 and didn't pitch one game in the minor leagues. He went directly into the majors. And...he did it with just one arm. It was amazing to watch him pitch."

"How do you know all about him?"

"Oh, duh, Dad! I know all about baseball and the players. I learned from the best!"

Terrence smiled and was about to hug his son when he heard a familiar voice coming from behind him. Someone gave Timothy a bear hug, squeezing him tight, and her feminine voice said, "Timothy, it's such a surprise to see you here."

"I didn't know you worked here, Mrs. Hernandez. I knew you were a nurse and worked in a hospital, but I didn't know which one. Luke never told me."

She smiled down at him. "We haven't seen you much lately and we sure do miss you. I heard about the train crash. I'm so sorry...if you ever—"

Terrence loudly cleared his throat to draw her attention. "*Dad* is sitting right here in the wheelchair. It's a big difference from our last confrontation." Terrence straightened up his back the best he could. A pained grunt escaped from his lips as he tried to turn in his chair and raise his hand. "Hello, you might not remember that my name is Terrence. Can we start over? I wanted to apologize for the other day, but as you can see, my life has thrown me a real curve ball." He rolled his eyes.

"That's okay, an apology isn't necessary. I could see you were in pain and I kind of overstepped my bounds by suggesting a physical therapist." Lacey ruffled Timothy's hair and then turned her attention back to Terrence. "What brings you to my neck of the woods?"

Timothy's face brightened up. "You work on this floor?"

"Yup.... I've been on this floor for a long time helping all of these wonderful patients get their lives back to normal."

"Is there ever a normal for all us gimps?" Everyone looked at Terrence and he stared back stubbornly.

"Normal...is what you make it. First of all, no one is perfect. Like that little one over there...." She pointed across the room. "She never had a chance. Her destiny was predetermined from birth. The blood from her legs was cut off from the umbilical cord that had wrapped around them. Doctors said she would never walk. But look at her now. She can do it all! Sometimes I even have a hard time keeping up with her." Lacey bent down and pulled up her pant leg to show a prosthetic right leg.

A shocked look registered across Terrence's face. She let her pant leg drop. She looked up, a faraway look on her face as she began to speak. "We had been in the mountains riding snowmobiles and having a blast. I was on the back of a powerful vehicle, holding on tight. The last thing I remember is my husband's contagious laugh as he pointed to a slight embankment. Only it wasn't just a slight mound. It was a twenty-five foot drop over a cliff. From that moment of impact, my life forever changed. Without going into the specifics, we flew through the air and the snowmobile landed on top of him. At the same time, my leg got caught and when we hit the ground, it was severed."

Terrence's eyes were open wide. "I'm so sorry...."

"There's no reason to be sorry for me. Everyone's lives are filled with moments that will change them forever. It's how you choose to deal with those sudden changes that will make the difference in your life. I had a baby and I needed to push myself forward. It wasn't just about me anymore. Just like this is not just about you...."

Unable to say much, Terrence barely mumbled out, "I know...."

"It's your turn to step up and teach your son some important values in life. He really looks up to you—don't disappoint him. You're alive. Take that as a plus and let's get you back into a good place."

Timothy and Vera were both standing there—speechless.

Lacey took ahold of the handles of the wheelchair and said casually, "I want to show you around so we can get your rehabilitation started."

Weeks later, Timothy and Luke were sitting in the cafeteria having lunch. It was the weekend and they both enjoyed coming down to visit Terrence and sneaking up on Lacey. Vera would drop them off and then come later to pick them up.

That morning in the car when she was about to drop off the boys, Vera said, "You're father is doing so well. He even got excited yesterday when the team called and offered him a position as an assistant coach as soon as he's out of rehab."

Timothy's grin covered his whole face. "Yes...he's doing great thanks to Mrs.

Hernandez! She's been a great inspiration to him."

Vera smirked, a bright twinkle in her eyes. "I think he may even be smitten with the young lady."

Luke tapped her shoulder from the backseat. "My mom is not so young. She's thirty-six!"

Vera started to laugh. "That's very young to me!"

Timothy shook his head. "You aren't old, Grandma."

She pulled up to the hospital and turned to them as they shut their doors. She opened the passenger window and called, "You keep an eye on those two...I don't want any hanky-panky!"

The boys nodded their heads and were laughing as the doors to the hospital opened.


Before the boys left that evening, they said goodbye to all of the friends they had made on the fourth floor. Terrence was using crutches and standing with his one leg.

Timothy hugged his father's hips. "I'm so proud of you, Pops!"

Terrence blushed. "I'm trying my hardest, Timothy."

Lacey walked up to Luke and gave him a big hug. She eyed the boys. "Did you get your homework done, guys?"

Timothy smirked. "Yes, ma'am."

She smiled. "Who would like to go out for a hamburger and milkshake?"

Both the boys began to jump up and down with gusto. "Can we go to the Hard Rock Café? I want to see my dad's picture on their wall."

"I guess we could...."

Terrence moved a step closer to Lacey and said, "I've been a good boy this week. Do you think I can come too?"

Lacey leaned into his shoulder. "You have been a good boy! Will your ego be able to take the picture of who you once were?"

He smiled. "Sure. I like who I am now...better!"

The group started walking toward the elevator.

# CHAPTER 15

## Enrique

In a small church nestled at the bottom of the Santa Monica Mountains, birds were chirping and a slight breeze ruffled the leaves of the old oak trees. The church was empty, except for one old man kneeling on the pew with his eyes closed and tears slowly sliding down his cheeks. His hands were clasped together and his mouth was muttering words that were inaudible. He had been coming to his church for months and sitting on the same pew, sometimes staring for hours at the old stained glass window as he prayed for forgiveness.

The stained glass window had been given to the church over fifty years ago. It had the most beautiful depiction of Jesus on the cross, splashing colors across the old plaster walls at the right time of day. The artistic glass had traveled from a small town in Mexico with a young husband and wife who left everything behind to start their new life. The only prized possession they brought with them was this wedding gift from a dear friend and artist that had lived in their village. It was the only thing of value they had to barter with when times got bad. Never once did they take the window out of the carefully packed bundle.

Years later, after they had settled into their new life and their family began to grow, they thought it was a privilege to donate the religious work of art to their church. The church had taken them under its wing and helped the young couple through some very difficult times. They had lived through the trials with no complaints.

Enrique and Maria loved their new country and the freedom of building a new life with honesty and integrity—values they handed down to their eight children.

Only once had Enrique fallen down onto his knees and begged for redemption and forgiveness. That was the day he lost his seven-year-old son to cancer. He was angry, as all parents would be after desperately seeking to save their innocent child. Maria and Enrique had done everything they could to save Jorge, but he was too sick, and even the best medical intervention would not have helped. For months, Enrique lingered in a deep depression, finding his only solace in his little church—talking to God and making peace with his loss. Now, here he was again, only this time his family was scared about his emotional breakdown. He was not the man he used to be, nor did he have the strength and ability to fully comprehend the loss of those aboard the train. Since the accident, he had burdened himself with tremendous guilt and responsibility for the crash. Though his family constantly reassured him that the accident was not his fault and that he had done the best he could to try to push his truck off the tracks, he continued to place the weight of the world on his old shoulders.

Every morning he woke up and went down to his church to pray for the families that had lost a loved one or the victims who endured painful injuries. He knew what the depth of sorrow loss could bring.

Quietly, the back door of the church opened and a tall figure stood in the doorway, blocking the light. His shoulders began to shake as he watched the old man pray. *Never before had he seen his father so broken.* Never before had he felt so helpless. Never before had he wished it was him to carry this burden of guilt. He slowly walked down the aisle until he reached the most important person in his life. He carefully slid into the pew and slipped his arm around his father's shaking shoulder. Enrique didn't acknowledged his son at all. His eyes were closed and he continued to mutter his desperate prayer.

Roberto leaned over and whispered, "Papa, you can't keep doing this to yourself." He sighed. "It wasn't your fault. We tried desperately to get your truck off that track. Nothing would budge it. Not even my heavy truck pushing from behind."

After several moments of deep silence, Enrique spoke. "My pain is so deep, my son. Watching the funerals from a distance and not being able to let the families know how deeply I grieve for them...."

"You could have gone to the funerals—"

"No! I was the source of all their pain!" His voice rose in anger.

"You were not!"

Enrique slammed his fist on the pew and grimaced. His shoulders began to tremble. Roberto pulled him close and held his head next to his heart as Enrique continued blaming himself.

He repeated over and over, *"Lo siento...* I'm sorry... so sorry...."

Roberto sat silently with his father for the next few hours, never leaving his side. Roberto was frightened at the diminishing size of his father as he wasted away from his self-imposed punishment.

Finally Roberto broke the silence. "I came down here to sit with you. I also wanted you to know that we got a call this morning from the NSTB. They are coming over this afternoon with the investigative report. They wanted us to see it."

Enrique didn't say a word. He just sat there and stared at the beautiful window.

Roberto reiterated his point. "You have to be there, Papa. They want you there. They requested that you be there."

Anger raised its ugly head as Enrique verbally attacked his son. "What for?" he yelled. He stood up and turned away from Roberto. "Everyone knows it was my truck that killed those innocent people. Are they coming to spit in my face?"

Roberto stood and grabbed his father's shoulders and screamed back, "They have some new information they wanted to relay to us, and they wanted to do it in person before the press gets ahold of it."

In a low whisper, Enrique said, "You get the information and come tell me. I want to stay here where I am safe from everything—including myself."

Roberto gazed at the broken man he loved so much. He said as gently as he could, "I will come get you in a few hours."

Enrique nodded and sat down. He then kneeled on his knees and began to pray.

Roberto opened the door to the church and noticed his father was not there. He began to panic as he looked around. His head was spinning as he muttered to himself, *"Where could he be? Where has he gone? He's not home and I drove here the same way he would walk. Please let him be okay...."*

He ran outside and searched the grounds, hoping to find his father. He screamed his name, "Papa...Papa...Papa...!"

A heavy hand came down on Roberto's shoulder. He spun around, hoping to see his father, but instead he was facing the priest of the church—Father Santiago. Wide-eyed, Roberto asked, "Is he still here? Where is he? Where did he go? If anything happens to him...."

The old Priest put his arm around Roberto's waist. "He's inside on one of the pews getting some sleep. I told him he needed some rest. You didn't see him, so I can understand your fear."

Roberto sighed in relief. He looked into the Priest's face. *"What can I do to help him through this? Should I be afraid he might do something to himself? Our family is distraught over his behavior and we don't know how to deal with it. Please tell me what to do? My mother is scared and worried...."*

Father Santiago nodded his head in understanding. "We talked. He just needs to spend some time letting go of his guilt. He knows deep down that it wasn't his fault, it's just hard to understand it. Your Papa is a loving man who put the deaths on his shoulders. I have faith something will change soon."

They eased over to the church doors. "I need to take him home. Can I ask a big favor? The NTSB is coming over in an hour and I don't know what they have to say. Can I call you to come over if it is bad news or he has a bad reaction?"

Father Santiago tapped his shoulder. "Sure, son."

An hour later, Roberto and his father walked into their modest home. It was clean and organized. Maria kept her house filled with all those things that had meant a lot to her—including her grandmother's rocking chair that had traveled with them from Mexico on one of their trips home to visit their families. Maria was sitting and knitting in her chair as she hummed a song and rocked back and forth.

Once the men entered the living room, Roberto asked, "Are we too late?"

Maria stopped rocking and shook her head. She stood up and placed her knitting on the chair that had rocked her through a lifetime of challenges. Nobody sat on her chair when her knitting was placed on the seat. They learned over the years that it had become her own sanctuary—her place of safety as life sent her challenging tribulations. She had rocked her way through eight pregnancies, her son's death, and so many more of life's hiccups.

She looked at her husband and walked over to take his hand. "They just called and said they would be here in a few minutes. Come on, Enrique, I have a surprise for you."

Roberto started to walk toward the front door. "I'm going to gather up whoever is here."

"I'm taking your father into the kitchen to feed him his favorite soup. I made my grandmother's *menudo rojo*. I know I usually only make it at New Years, but I think this is going to be a good day."

Enrique didn't say a word, he just followed his wife into the kitchen. Step by step, he dragged his old and tired legs across the hardwood floors.

As Maria opened the kitchen door, Roberto witnessed the first grin to cross his father's face in the last two months.

Roberto inhaled a deep breath and thought how a cup of soup could always do that to his dad. *I guess I never developed a taste for menudo. I think it was just the thought of using veal knuckles, cow's feet, and the lining of a cow's stomach that turned me off. None of that sounds the least bit appetizing!*

Roberto headed out of the front door. For the past few months, life around their household had been very solemn and everyone seemed to keep their distance. The men were out in the field for longer stretches of time and the women stayed sequestered in the kitchen, more out of fear that they would say or do something to upset their tormented father than anything else.

The NTSB and FRA had done a thorough investigation into the crash. Their conclusion of the report was going to be announced on the evening news. They thought it only fair that Enrique and his family should be the first to hear it. They had scoured the crash site for months and had examined Enrique's truck in order to determine the exact cause of the crash. Everything was taken into consideration, including the braking system of the train and the speed in which it had been traveling. It had taken the agencies over two months to accumulate all of the facts from that morning and what lead up to the impact. Roberto prayed that their new information would be a comfort to his father.

Roberto stood outside in the yard with his brothers Edwardo, Juan, and Pedro. He turned and said, "I hope those reports don't put all of the blame on Papa. I'm afraid that would crush his spirit completely."

Juan crossed his hands over his chest as a sign of affirmation. "We already know it was the truck on the track that created the crash. What more could it be?"

Pedro spoke up with a powerful voice. "Many things! For one, it could have been partly due to a faulty warning signal to the train engineer. Or maybe the speed of the locomotive was too fast, making it unable to stop in time. You know there is an ordinance for the speed of the trains in certain residential areas. Or maybe the engineer wasn't paying attention to the warnings because he was texting or resting." His eyes narrowed. "You do know that texting is what caused the crash in Chatsworth a few years back. He should have shut off his phone. He missed the blinking light on the track!"

Roberto looked miserable with worry. "You're right, Pedro. There could be a number of things that could add up to cause a crash of this caliber. Whatever the outcome, we will deal with it."

Roberto and Juan nodded. Pedro was right. There could have been mitigating circumstances that contributed to the crash as well. Or, they could blame the entire crash on the truck. It was a coin toss at this point. The three men walked slowly to the house to lend their support to their parents.

The men walked into the kitchen and sat down with their father at the table. He had just finished his meal and was sipping a cup of coffee.

Roberto spoke first, compassion in his voice. "Papa, we know your grief and the responsibility you feel. Whatever is said today...your family stands behind you. We will think of some way to contact the families with our deepest respect for their loss and offer them whatever we can."

"I watched from across the street of that church when they buried the young woman. Her family was beyond heartache. She was to be married that day and all their dreams had been stolen. How do you pay for that? How do you give them back their lifetime of dreams? I'm not a rich man, but if money would make their pain stop...."

There was a sudden knock at the front door.

The kitchen became so quiet they could hear the breeze rustling through the Eucalyptus trees. Roberto stood up and walked out of the kitchen and into the living room to the front door. He greeted the three men and one woman and led them into the room. Enrique and Maria walked into the living room holding hands, Pedro and Juan on their heels. Introductions were made and everyone took a seat. On one side of the room sat Enrique and his family, and at the other, the judges who were about to read the verdict.

The door opened and a man walked in, carrying a heavy box in his arms. It was five feet long and a two feet deep. He tried not to drag the box across the floor. When he took a seat, he placed the box next to his chair, positioning it upward.

Roberto stood up. "Before any of you say anything, I want you to know how terrible our family feels and how deeply hurt my father is. You need to know he tried his hardest to get his truck off the tracks— nothing freed the front tires. The media has made him into a villain and the hate mail and harassment has been nonstop. I don't let him onto the computer, because the circulating innuendo has been very hurtful. If you are here to strike us down, please take into consideration that my father is old and his heart just can't take much more. "

The spokesperson for the group stood up and nodded. "We know that, Roberto. We are here to let you know all the facts that we found and hopefully bring a form of solace back into your lives. Everyone needs that right now."

"Thank you. I know there is nothing you can say that will bring back the lives lost. We just want everyone to know that nothing was done with intent to hurt or maim anyone. My father has been a respected pillar in our community and now he feels he is on trial."

The spokesman nodded to Enrique. "We are here to let you know that nothing could have gotten that old truck off the track."

"Nothing...I don't understand...." Roberto looked confused.

Fear of what was to come forced Enrique to put his hands over his face and he began to silently weep.

Roberto place his hand on his father's back, and then he bent down and said, "I love you, Papa. It wasn't your fault and we will get through this."

The man with the box stood up as well. "We know why your father's truck would not move. We came here out of respect for him and your family. We wanted your family to be the first to hear the truth before the media goes wild with the information and twists it back into lies and rumors again. You needed the truth." He opened the box and pulled out a five-foot long strip of steel with sharp spikes across the entire length. It looked more dangerous than a great white shark.

"This was placed on the track in a very strategic way so that it would tear deep into the tires of a car or truck that drove over it. Once that happened...the tires became locked, in a sense, to the track. Unfortunately, it was deliberately put there with the intention of creating this crash. We now know that. We have a lead as to who committed this heinous act, but are not allowed to say anything until the suspect is picked up."

The silence in the room was deafening. After the shock began to wear off, Enrique's sobs tore through the room. Maria hugged her husband tight as he slowly let go of all the emotional weight he had been carrying since the day of the crash.

The Gomez family was stunned. No one said a word. Everyone looked at each other as though the heavy albatross had been lifted off all of their shoulders.

The spokesman added, "I know this comes as a shock, but it does take 'all' the responsibility off of your father and his truck. We came to let you know that nothing...and I mean nothing...could have prevented the crash. All of the details are in this report." He stepped forward and handed Roberto a large manila envelope and slapped him on the back. "We hope this brings peace and closure to your family. This breaking news will be aired tonight. They will get a look at this strip with metal spikes. All the media has been contacted. If there is anything you need or that we can do...please do not hesitate to call." He handed Roberto a card and shook his hand. "Thank you. Our investigation is officially over. I hope we will all be able to sleep peacefully tonight and that those who did this heinous act will be caught and prosecuted."

"My entire family thanks you for coming to us first with this," Roberto said.

The group started to walk out the door when the man turned and said, "When you watch the news tonight, don't be surprised at anything. That is all I can say. And please do not let anyone know. All will be exposed tonight."

# EPILOGUE

## One year later....

In that one moment of impact when the train barreled into the truck, everyone's lives changed. There was no rhyme or reason for who survived and who died. It was just an unfortunate accident that took the lives of so many loved ones. The injured survived, but not without permanent scars that will be with them and their loved ones forever. Their lives were altered, and moving forward is a very long and difficult journey of healing.

Today, the mood was somber, but the sun was shining over the large crowd starting to gather near the chairs. Many had shown up for the one year anniversary presentation in honor of those who were lost and injured in the Metrolink train crash. Doctors, nurses, triage, first responders, law enforcement, and firemen came to see the progress of those who had survived and to acknowledge those who hadn't. They were standing in the front row, waiting for the ceremony to begin.

Yellow tape had been placed around the area and no one was allowed in except the invited guests. The rest of the crowd, filled with bystanders and reporters, had to stand behind the yellow line. The mayor and city officials were not going to allow a circus-like atmosphere to invade this poignant occasion. They wanted the victims and the emergency personnel to be respected for their courage and hard work.

Chase was there with his sons. Bridget chose not to come. Terrence brought his fiancé Lacey, who was an instrumental part of his rehabilitation, and he was now walking on a new prosthetic. Timothy and Luke were there to lend emotional support to his father. Karyn was wearing a pretty summer dress and sitting next to Penny and Kane. Yun and her brother, Chun, looked healthy and happy. Katy grinned at her two best friends. José and his mother, Maria, were hurriedly walking down the aisle, Assandro and his wife following behind.

Soft music was drifting across the area from the PA system and the strong fragrance of fresh flowers permeated the air. A large draped sheet was hanging across the new memorial, waiting for the unveiling.

Off to the left side, there was a private section of chairs where the families of the deceased sat. There were pictures of each of those lost in the crash perched on a pedestal surrounded by flowers.

The fourth picture was Harper Puzzio-Lewis. Austin had made sure she had his last name posted. The Puzzio family was seated and waiting quietly. Hilary looked at her mother and could see she was visibly unsettled by all the people. Tears were slowly sliding down her cheeks. Nico Puzzio placed his arm around his wife's shoulders and pulled her closer. Her shoulders began to shake.

The Lewis family had just arrived and Austin approached the Puzzios and gave each of them a hug and then walked up to Harper's photograph and placed a bouquet of wild flowers. The audience quieted down as they watched him carefully brush a tear from his face as he placed another picture of Harper up on the pedestal.

In the very back row sat a quiet Hispanic family. Enrique and his wife were holding hands. In Maria's hand was her mother's rosary beads that she continued to rub. Roberto and his siblings were waiting for the service to begin.

The man at the podium tapped the microphone, drawing the attention of the crowd. Everyone sat down and their eyes were riveted on the speaker. He said, "I want to thank you all for coming today. At this time, I would like to introduce you to Mr. Layland, the CEO of Metrolink."

The two men shook hands and the first walked to the side of the stage.

"Good morning. As you know, we are here to honor those we lost, the injured, and all of the triage and emergency personnel. On that beautiful day in June, a malicious act was perpetrated on hundreds of unsuspecting Metrolink passengers, causing deaths, injuries, mass destruction...and leaving in its wake a veritable ocean of pain and sorrow. Four young men purposely and willfully attached a strip of steel filled with iron spikes to flatten the tires of a vehicle and create an inevitable collision. This tragic act has changed the lives of all of us here today. Unfortunately, Enrique Gomez, whose truck stuck to the track, became the recipient of this senseless and cruel joke. His family was devastated and heartbroken and he has personally funded the new emergency alert system that goes directly to the engineer and the Metrolink, so that this can never happen again."

He pulled off the sheet and began to say, "We would like to thank...."

Everyone stood up to get a better look at the striking bronze statue of two children holding a plaque. On the plaque were the names of those who had died. Without a thought as to what he was doing, Austin stood, picked a wildflower, and approached the memorial. He looked to the sky and then gently placed the stem in front of the statue. The entire audience began forming a single file line as each person placed a flower before the memorial....

In one moment of impact, lives
change forever and there is no
going back to before. As much as
we try or do not want to...we must
always continue to take small steps
forward. This pushes us to move
through the pain and sorrow, for if
we lose the will to live...we lose
that chance for a new beginning.

~*Rene d. Schultz*

I love to garden, try new recipes, take lots of pictures, and occasionally I enjoy a glass of wine with dear friends. I've never jumped out of a plane, climbed Mt. Everest, or seen the Northern Lights of Alaska. But, I have danced in the rain, sent a message in a bottle, and I've rode my motorcycle down the Pacific Coast Highway on sunny California days!

My passion for writing has led me on the most amazing journey. I thrive on developing strong storylines that showcase today's contemporary lifestyles. Rags to riches, Robin Hood, and surviving the odds seem to be my common denominators that showcase my fascinating and diverse characters.

# BOOKS BY

## RENE D. SCHULTZ

# OVER 150 TOTAL 5-STAR
# REVIEWS ON AMAZON!

RENE HAS GAINED THE LOYALTY
OF SO MANY READERS, AND
WITH GOOD REASON.

HER BOOKS ARE REAL,
COMPELLING, AND A TRUE
TESTAMENT TO THE WORLD WE
LIVE IN TODAY.

REALITY FICTION.
THAT'S JUST HOW SHE ROLLS.


# REALITY FICTION.
## REALLY GOOD FICTION.

# DONE DEAL

Done Deal is an inspiring book about a woman who doesn't understand why the pharmaceuticals are holding back 'orphan' drugs that can save lives. Why insurance companies won't pay to keep people alive. And why the government is closing its 'blind eyes.' Cissy goes on a quest to find these answers and what she discovers is shocking. With an anger that leaves her cynical, and with time running out, she sets out to 'right a wrong.' She forfeits her integrity and leaves a legacy that will crush the greedy pharmaceuticals and the corrupt insurance companies!

With the new age of technology, hackers become a reality and new Robin Hoods emerge.

# BISHOP STREET

Bishop Street is an emotional, gut-wrenching journey of survival, friendship, and second chances....

After twenty years, Maggie makes a life-changing decision to find her three best friends from the orphanage in which she grew up.

From the small towns in North Dakota, across the exotic beaches in Mexico, to searching the streets and homeless shelters of Los Angeles...will she find more than just her long-lost friends?

# HOUSE OF STONE

The greatly anticipated sequel to Bishop Street, new adventures await Maggie and loved ones.

Challenging themselves to let go of the past, and still fused together by the immeasurable power of friendship, Maggie, Elizabeth, Lucy, and Randolph are back together....

Unexpectedly, their lives will change forever when Maggie is visiting an orphanage in Honduras. A major earthquake hits. Thousands of lives of lost, Maggie is missing, and their worst fears will test their strength, once again.

# BROKEN IMAGE

Seeing images of flawless females on television, magazines, movies, and on the internet makes it hard for women—or anyone—to feel good about their bodies and themselves. Mercedes knew she was not beautiful, or stunning, or even close to either. She was plain, simple, and ordinary. Having survived a dysfunctional childhood that left scars on her already shaky self-esteem, she was stronger than she realized.

Take this journey with Mercedes as she faces decisions that will change her life forever.

# IF I COULD...

At nineteen, Ema Vaduva was pregnant when she was forced to leave Romania. For twenty-eight years, Ema and her daughter, Daniela, lived a modest and reclusive life. They were inseparable until one fatal day—Ema died. That day would change Dani's life forever.

She had never been all alone and had no family to call her own. One afternoon while cleaning out her mother's closet, she finds a brown box. Are the secrets to her mother's past tucked inside?

Feeling alone and desperate, and with nothing else to lose, Dani goes in search of answers. Will that brown box hold the answers to Ema's past and Dani's future...?

Please leave an honest review of *Moment of Impact* on Amazon and Goodreads. I appreciate the feedback and the sacrifice of your time so much.

Yours forever,

Rene D. Schultz